DANGER'S EDGE

JAY .H. DEE

Cover Photos by Jo Verhoef, and Yeko Photo Studio (Depositphotos).
Cover design by Jay .H. Dee, Victoria, Australia.

Danger's Edge

ISBN 978-0-9942436-5-2

Dedicated to
my husband Bright.
I love you so much!

ACKNOWLEDGEMENTS

I just want to take a moment to say thank you to my family and friends for their ongoing support. I know I always say this, but your love and encouragement are what keep me pursuing this dream.

A special thanks to Jo Verhoef for her invaluable help with the cover pictures. Special thanks also to Yanina, Karen, Rachel and Eva for your input, friendship and for sharing my excitement each time I accomplish a new goal and publish another book. I don't think you'll ever know how much that has meant.

And finally to Lynne, my mum and my biggest fan. You're the best mum a girl could ever ask for. Without you, none of these books would ever get off the ground. I love you so much!

PROLOGUE

An inch either way was death. Laina marveled that the youth had survived. She abseiled the last few yards to his position, gentle with each push off the rock wall, lest she dislodge loose stones that might fall on the teen.

"Jake, if you can hear me, stay very still." She secured her position with two anchors into a small crevice just above the boy. Laina sat in her harness at his level and assessed the situation.

The teenager was precariously lying on a thin ledge fifteen feet below the gorge lip. He and his buddy had apparently attempted to cross using the old fallen log. Laina sighed. She had done it countless times as a teen. However, time had rotted the log and a chunk had clearly given way beneath the boy's foot. Now here he lay, lucky he hadn't plunged the last twenty feet into the icy rapids, but also unlucky to have knocked himself unconscious.

At a glance, Laina could tell Jake's right leg was broken. The bone just below the knee was jutting out against the skin, but thankfully had not protruded. The left side of his face was grazed and starting to bruise where he had obviously collided with the rock wall on his way down. The collision had caused him to twist and land on his right side. His left arm and leg were dangling from the ledge. He had only to arouse and make the slightest movement and he would fall.

Aware there could be possible spinal injuries, Laina decided to call for backup. He would need to be immobilized before being airlifted. She removed the two-way radio clipped to her first aid backpack and keyed the mic.

"Gaz, tell the chopper on standby we need them for an extraction ASAP. Then I'll need your help when the chopper arrives."

"Roger that."

Laina got to work securing the boy and splinting his leg. She worked calmly and with efficiency. Less than five minutes later, her partner Gary, a man of about forty, abseiled slowly down to provide assistance. They worked steadily together. It wasn't long before the sound of pounding rotor blades bounced off the surrounding mountains.

Like a large bird of prey, the rescue helicopter reached their position and commenced a hover. A basket stretcher was lowered out of an open door and Laina and Gary, with practiced movements, maneuvered the boy first onto a backboard and then into the rescue apparatus. His eyes fluttered and opened just as Laina tightened the last strap. Jake's cloudy, confused gaze met her clear blue eyes and she smiled assurance.

"Hang in there. The rescue chopper is about to pull you up and take you to hospital. You're going to be just fine."

The tiniest glimmer of a smile tugged at the boy's lips a moment before the helicopter began reeling the basket stretcher upward, causing a groan of pain. Laina watched it go, hoping that she was right. Who knew the extent to which the fall had injured the boy? There was the distinct possibility of a head injury and also internal bleeding. Laina glanced at her partner who met her gaze gravely. He too appeared to be thinking the same thing.

"Come on." Gary zipped her pack shut and helped her shoulder it. "We get off shift in half an hour. May as well drop into Walkerville hospital and find out how Jake is doing."

Laina was all for it and her grin said as much. "Race you to the top?"

Gary rolled his eyes but still mounted every last drop of energy and skill to beat her. He took off up the rock wall with smooth movements. Laina laughed and followed.

1

"Hey Gaz, pull over here will you?" Laina's gaze locked on a building site not far from the Walkerville hospital. Her eyes and smile were instantly alight.

Gary appeared momentarily puzzled. "Here?" He pulled to the curb behind a red Ford pickup.

Laina gave him a distracted smiling glance and reached for the door handle. "Thanks."

"Are you sure you don't want a ride back to Icy Creek?"

Laina pointed to a strapping young man in jeans and a checkered shirt pounding nails into a house frame twenty yards from the curb. "I'll ride home with Logan."

Gary studied the young builder through the windshield, his expression inscrutable. "I didn't know you had a boyfriend."

Laina frowned at the calm comment. She had only known Gary a few months since her assignment to the Walkerville rescue paramedics division. They worked well together, however never spent time socializing outside of work.

"I don't. We're just friends." Laina unbuckled her seatbelt. "See you tomorrow." She cast her coworker a smile and got out of their work vehicle.

Gary smiled and waved before pulling away from the curb. She turned to the building site and strode toward her friend. Logan was just reaching for the nail box on a sawhorse beside him and must have noticed movement. He glanced over his shoulder, spotted Laina and a wide smile broke across his face. He slotted his hammer into his tool belt and stood with hands on his hips as she approached.

"Hi Ace! What are you doing on my turf?"

Laina's heart lifted with his cheerful greeting. "Just got off shift and checked on a boy we rescued after lunch. He fell off that log over the gorge we used to cross when we were kids."

A look of genuine concern furrowed his brow. "Is he okay? Those rapids are brutal."

Laina stopped and sat on the sawhorse beside him. "A few broken bones, concussion and a seriously wounded ego." She gestured to the almost completed house frame. "How about you? How long till this job is finished?"

Logan blew out his cheeks. "A while. Every time I knock up a wall, the owner goes and changes the floor plan. A door here, a cupboard there." He grinned at her and shrugged. "What can I do? I'm getting paid, so he ought to be happy with what he gets."

Laina marveled at his patient response. When she had first met him after she'd just moved to Icy Creek, Logan had been renowned for his bad attitude and temper. At sixteen, he had begun a relationship with

Jesus Christ, which had radically impacted his life. Now twenty-six, the changes were remarkable.

"Are you headed home soon?"

Logan surveyed his work and finally turned a smile on her. "I'm thinking pizza. You?"

"I was thinking more along the lines of burgers and fries."

Logan chuckled and began packing up his equipment. "I'll be in that. Give me a few minutes." He took his keys from his pocket and tossed them to her.

Laina caught them.

"Why don't you wait in the truck? It's cold out."

"You still got my favorite CD in there?" She stood.

Logan ruffled her hair. "What else would I be listening to with you around all the time?"

Laina poked her tongue out at him and dodged when he reached to swat her arm.

* * *

"I was right all those years ago," Logan mumbled as he watched her saunter happily toward his pickup, aware she could no longer hear him. "You are trouble."

He drank in the sight of her for one moment and smiled to himself. He shook his head and finished gathering his tools and began packing them into the tool chest bolted to the tray of his truck.

Laina's favorite artist was already blaring from the stereo inside the cab. A sense of contented enjoyment nestled around his soul. He whispered a prayer of thanks for life as it was, unaware it was about to alter irrevocably.

* * *

Zach saved the final changes and made a copy of the new tablet application he had created. It was time for testing. He removed the software and closed down his computer, shutting off the light on his way out of his office. It was also time to go home.

With a sigh, he wandered into his manager's office and dropped the USB on his desk. The room was empty, as was the rest of the building. It was ten pm and he had promised to finish the job tonight. He was weary of such high pressure for something as unimportant as a computer application.

He'd been given the opportunity to design some apps for the new device his boss' company had produced. It had been a little more high profile than his usual projects. However, he could not shake the restless feeling in his spirit. Was he really making a difference in the world by making Computer Software? Was that even possible to do? Yes, it was. But was he making a difference? He doubted it.

Zach took the elevator to the basement parking lot and found his car. It wasn't hard to do seeing as it was the only one there. Once out in New York traffic, it was difficult to believe it was ten at night. The city was still alive and kicking as though it was seven in the morning.

A moment of longing for the quiet streets of Icy Creek hit him squarely in the chest. He headed for the pretentious restaurant where he knew his girlfriend was waiting. Finding a parking space only served to fuel his discontent. One hour and twenty minutes later than he should have, Zach walked in.

Soft lighting from crystal chandeliers dropped a gentle ambience over the mahogany furniture and tables draped in white linen. Even at this hour the room was packed. However, only the gentle hum of conversation and the tinkle of utensils on fine china could be heard. It was a vast contrast to the bright lights of city traffic and blaring horns and curses of impatient drivers.

Zach spotted her sitting at a small table in the center of the room perusing a menu. He paused in the archway between reception and the dining area. Gorgeous brunette curls framed her perfect features. An elegant cocktail dress of blue satin shimmered in the soft lighting. She was beautiful, and she was his.

Why didn't that thought fill him with joy? He shook off the dark mood that had settled over him and approached her, determined to enjoy the one good thing in his life on this dismal day.

Brylie Montgomery glanced up as he neared her table and her face lit with a delighted smile. "Zach! When you called and said you would be late I had no idea." She smiled and stood to plant a kiss on his cheek.

Zach accepted it and held her chair for her to be seated again. "Yeah, I'm sorry about that. The software took longer to complete than I thought it would." He took a seat and picked up his menu. He was starved.

"Oh don't apologize." She waved him aside, her smile still in place. "That's a good thing."

Zach frowned and looked at her over his menu. She was pleased he was late for their date? "Pardon?"

Brylie caught his baffled gaze. "You're working hard which will make your boss happy. A happy boss and great products lead to promotion. Hang in there."

The dark mood descended again. Why did that logic bother him so much? He shoved it aside and concentrated on the menu. Great! It was in French.

The longing for home hit him again, only stronger this time. What he wouldn't give to be in Gracie's humble diner with fries and a burger on his plate, surrounded by Nick, Wil, Logan and Laina. Although rare and a long time in between, the feeling of homesickness helped to make up his mind. Tomorrow he would request a few days off and fly home for a visit.

* * *

Jamison Harlan filed onto the bus with his fellow inmates, watched closely by a hard faced guard by the door with a pump action shot gun. Another stood behind the line of prisoners destined for transport. His mind was racing. They were headed for prison where they would await the inevitable trial. What worried him most was Vince.

Jamison studied his partner surreptitiously out of the

corner of his eye as he was shackled to his seat. He was too cocky for someone facing jail time. Jamison steeled himself for trouble as the last prisoners were loaded and secured. At least he was holding all the cards.

The engine sputtered to life and within minutes the bus was underway, weaving its way toward the county lock up.

* * *

Logan smiled to himself as he drove to his mom's house. He had just dropped Laina at her place after a great evening at Gracie's diner, laughing and talking about every topic under the sun.

His heart soared, as it usually did whenever he spent time with her. It made the mundane task of fixing his mom's backed up plumbing a breeze. He pulled to the curb outside her house and his curiosity peaked. A strange car was in the driveway. Who would be visiting his mother at this hour?

As he approached the front door, he could hear conversation inside. A familiar male voice sent a shiver down his spine. Although everything seemed calm, Logan was unconvinced it would stay that way. He entered and stood quietly in the doorway between the hall and the den, assessing the situation.

Walter Mathews sat on a faded blue armchair facing his wife Anne. She was on the sofa beside their autistic daughter, Tia.

"And when did this happen?" she was asking, her expression open.

"Three weeks ago. I met a man at work who told me about what Jesus did. Rick's a good guy and his life shows that this Christianity thing is for real. I wanted it for myself." Walter wrapped his fingers around a hot mug of coffee.

Logan was astonished at what he was hearing, and a little skeptical. Anne spotted him in the doorway and her gaze alerted Walter to their son's presence. He turned in his chair and had to have noticed the calculated gaze leveled on him. He sat his mug aside and stood.

Walter extended his hand in greeting. Logan glanced between his father's outstretched hand and the man himself. He hesitated and slowly the hand returned to Walter's side. The welcoming smile left.

A flood of memories assaulted Logan, all of them nasty scenes that had played out in this very room. Fists flying, cussing, and the tears... They were what haunted him most.

And then there was that last time when he'd stood between his mother who lay beaten on the floor, and his father who wanted to go a second round. Logan had finally developed the physical power to give as good as he got. He'd sent his dad sprawling with a wicked right hook and swore that if Walter ever returned, he would do it again, or worse. The moment had come.

The words that sprang from his lips were cool, and his gaze measured. "Why are you here?"

Contrition and humility came over Walter's demeanor. "I'm here to put things right and to apologize for how I treated you and your mom all those years ago."

Logan was stunned. His father had never apologized in his whole life. An uncomfortable silence fell over the room. What was he supposed to say? Forgiveness was not an option, but trust? The Holy Spirit prompted Logan's heart and he chose to obey.

"I forgave you long ago, Dad." He sighed and ran a hand through his hair. "In fact, I should probably apologize for the hateful stuff I said back then."

Walter's brows rose in surprise. Logan realized he was not the boy his father remembered. Anne's tension eased and she smiled.

"We've been discussing your father moving back in."

Logan's heart froze in his chest. "No."

A frown furrowed Anne's brow and Walter looked astounded.

"Didn't you hear what I've been telling your mom? I-"

"I know, you said you've had a life changing experience." Logan glanced at his sister twirling a feather in her fingers, her eyes averted toward the far wall. Her free hand gripped her knee in agitation. She didn't need to be silent witness to any more violence. "I want to see the changes before I trust you again with my family." Logan looked at his father squarely.

A flicker of something Logan did not like entered his father's eyes.

"You talk like you're the man of this house."

"For a long time that's what I've had to be."

"This decision is for your mother and me," Walter reminded him curtly.

"You're right about this decision being between you and mom, but if I so much as hear a cuss word out of you toward her or see a single bruise, you'll wish you never came back." There was no malice in Logan's words, only protectiveness. He knew this man, or at least who he used to be.

Walter's voice softened in contrition. "I've changed, son."

Logan held eye contact and felt compassion. "I truly hope so, Dad. You just need to give us some time while you prove it."

"And what do you think, Anne?" Walter turned to her, his expression saying he knew she would side with him. She always had.

Anne hesitated. Logan had made a very good point and he understood the peace she had experienced for the last eleven years. He had too. He hoped it was too precious to risk after one positive evening. She looked between father and son.

"I think Logan is right." She held her husband's stunned gaze. "Come for dinner in the evenings, Walt, and spend time with us, but let's not rush this."

Logan inwardly sagged with relief. However, the honest disappointment in his father's face was almost too much for him. An unearthly compassion came over him. "Have you got a place to stay?"

Walter's dejected eyes fell upon his son. "No."

"You can stay with me till you find your feet. The lumber yard has jobs going if you're interested in sticking around, and the town has plenty of places to rent."

Walter looked stunned, and humbled enough to accept. "Thanks son."

"I'll fix the kitchen sink and then I'm headed home to sleep. You can follow me in your car." Logan moved toward the kitchen as he spoke.

No one could miss the fact the last statement was an order.

"Another coffee? That one's gone cold," Anne's soft voice followed him into the kitchen.

"No, but thanks anyway. It seems the boy is in a hurry."

2

Deputy Nick Foster was assessing the scene when the ambulances arrived. It was only an hour or so before dawn and pitch-black darkness pressed in around the edges of the floodlights provided by the county police department. They now illuminated the crash site. He was not surprised to see Laina emerge from the first ambulance followed by her partner.

Three other ambulances pulled in behind them against the steep embankment behind the fire truck. Their teams disembarked.

The winding mountain road had been carved into the hillside. To the left, the embankment stretched toward the heavens. To the right, a steep decline covered in shrubbery and dotted with the occasional cluster of trees sank into the valley below. This was one treacherous stretch of highway.

Laina trotted to his side. "Hey Nick, what have we got?"

He pointed to the bus suspended on a boulder twenty yards below the road. It was buckled and had clearly seen better days. The shouts and moaning of terrified, injured passengers filled the predawn air.

"A prison transport ran off the road. Fire fighters are

trying to cut them loose from the wreck before it loses stability and slides the rest of the way down the mountain. We haven't got the equipment to stabilize it."

"No one has a snap strap or chain to anchor the bus to a tree or something?" Laina followed him down the slope.

"It's a bus. Nothing we've got will hold it. The tow truck is our best bet. It's on route, but by the looks of it, it won't make it in time."

"And the passengers? How are they?" Laina watched her footing on the steep hillside. They half slid, half scrambled the twenty yards to the precariously balanced bus.

"They're pretty banged up. Three are dead, including one of the two guards."

Nick set to work assisting alongside others from both the fire and county police departments. Laina joined the ambulance teams who were beginning triage, as the emergency crews extricated prisoners one by one from the wreckage.

The seriously injured were hauled carefully by stretcher to the waiting ambulances above, while others were helped to the road on foot and treated there under guard.

Laina made her final trip down to help with the remaining passengers. She passed two firemen who were starting up the slope carrying a wounded man from the wreck.

"Hey, is anyone out there? I need help with this last guy!" an urgent shout came from inside the bus.

Laina glanced up the incline. Three ambulances had left already and the fourth was waiting for the last two patients. Gary was at the top of the hill assisting with a serious head injury and most county police were tied up with the prisoners. Several firemen and deputies were starting back down, but they were too far away to be of assistance, and there was no time to wait.

Laina listened to the telltale slipping noise of metal on rock and adrenaline hit her. The bus was minutes from its final decent down the slope. She climbed carefully onto its side as it lay wedged against the boulder. Its tail pulled it down another foot and her heart hammered in her chest. Urgent shouts from within spurred her next action.

She dropped through the open doorway to the 'floor'. Shattered glass against window mesh crunched under her feet. It seemed bizarre to be walking along the row of windows, stepping over seats to reach the back. There a fireman was using bolt cutters to break the last chain from the prisoner's feet.

The man lay curled against the window mesh. Blood partially covered his right cheek from a nasty head injury. It was difficult to assess other damage inflicted by the accident due to the poor lighting. Only a headlamp attached to the fireman's helmet lit the interior.

"What's your name?" Laina asked the prisoner with a calm she did not feel.

Brown eyes clouded by pain met hers. "Jamison Harlan." The words were slurred.

"Do you have movement of your fingers and toes?"

Even if there was a spinal injury, time was critical and preserving his life took priority.

"Yes."

"And your neck and back... any pain or tingling?"

"No. Just my head." He winced as the chains were severed that bound his hands to his feet and his feet to the bolt in the floor.

"Alright, he's free. Help me carry him past these seats to the door." The fireman discarded the bolt cutters.

Between the two of them, they lifted the injured man. Laina carried his feet, while the fireman took the bulk of his weight by holding him beneath the arms. It was not ideal. The bus shifted again, its tail slipping several more feet.

"Go! Go! Go!" she urged. They stepped over the mesh dividing the passengers from the driver's seat. She knew she would not be strong enough to lift the man's deadweight. "Get out and pull him up!" She held Jamison upright by propping herself under his shoulder and circling his waist with her hands, while the fireman climbed out.

"Take this." Jamison gripped her right hand. She glanced down. It was a scrap of scrunched, bloodied paper.

"We've got to get you out of here." She tried to maneuver him directly beneath the open doorway above them. The fireman's feet disappeared.

"Take it!" Jamison insisted and squeezed her hand tighter, visibly struggling against dizziness.

Without thinking, Laina took the paper and dropped it into her jacket pocket. Metal groaned ominously. A pair of hands reached back down through the doorway. Laina held one of Jamison's arms aloft and he was unceremoniously hauled upward. She pushed his legs free and gripped the handrails either side of the entrance.

Metal shrieking and scraping propelled her movements and she pulled herself up. She caught sight of Jamison's legs once again as he was dragged off the bus and onto solid ground. More voices joined the fireman's as others rushed to provide assistance. The wreckage twisted slowly until the tail was completely facing the slope.

Laina scrambled out and came to her feet on the side of the bus as it began sliding free of the boulder. She leapt clear with all of her might and felt the bus disappear from beneath her. It picked up speed down the slope and began rolling. The loud sounds of buckling metal and shattering glass brought the crash site to a horrified halt.

Laina's feet landed on steep terrain and she lost balance, falling to her left and tumbling in the wake of the wreckage. Panic, adrenaline and fear chased through her in quick succession, brought to an abrupt end by a teeth jarring thud into a tree. Her mind exploded in pain. Her lungs refused to draw breath and panic returned in full force.

* * *

"You just did what?" Brylie's voice hissed over the line.

Zach sat back in his desk chair, his cell phone to his ear. His excitement quickly fizzled out. "It's just for a week. I kind of hoped you might like to come over the weekend."

"Zach, all of your hard work and overtime will be for nothing!"

He frowned in bewilderment. "What are you talking about?"

"Promotion. Your boss needs to see that nothing comes before your work. If you start taking days off, he'll see you're not serious and he'll give more responsibility to someone else."

Zach was puzzled. What was really going on here? "So are you saying you won't come?"

There was a lengthy pause on the other end of the line. "I have a deadline to meet for a really big portfolio."

Disappointment lodged around Zach's heart. He had hoped to introduce her to his mom. He supposed he had only himself to blame. He had sprung the trip on her with little time to plan. "Alright then. I guess I'll call you when I get there." He sounded as dejected as he felt.

"Have a safe flight."

The line disconnected before he could wish her well concerning her deadline. Her tone had been cool. She was angry with him. Zach shook his head and sat his phone aside on his desk. He had work to do if he was to take some vacation time in a couple of days, which was why he had come to work so early in the morning.

Things weren't working out as he had planned, however he refused to allow that to keep him from going home for a visit. He had come to think of Icy Creek as his hometown, and he missed it something fierce.

* * *

Torchlight blinded Laina and she squinted to see the face bending over her. It was the same fireman who had pulled Jamison from the wreck.

"You are one brave lady!" He knelt at her side. "Anything broken?"

Laina groaned and sat up. "I guess we'll soon see. Is he okay?"

The fireman understood her reference to their patient. "He's out, but whether he'll be alright is something for a doctor to answer. Let's get you up the hill. You look like you could do with an ambulance yourself." He placed a hand under her right arm to help her to her feet.

Laina clenched her teeth against the soreness in her ribs and the searing pain in her upper left arm, which had taken the brunt of the collision. Once standing, her world began to spin. She reached out her good arm to steady herself against the offending tree.

"Name's Laina by the way." A small smile of irony appeared.

The fireman chuckled. "Rick. Good to meet you."

The sound of voices shouting and approaching foot-steps filled the early morning air as the remaining emergency crew arrived to offer assistance.

"You're a good man to have around in a sticky situation." Laina forced leaden feet to carry her up the hill-side one small step at a time.

Rick grinned, and seeing that she was able to walk unassisted, trotted quickly back toward Jamison. "You're not so bad yourself," he tossed over his shoulder. "I'm gonna kill my partner for leaving me in there alone!"

Laina shook her head at her close brush with death and slowly picked her way to the top on legs made of jello.

* * *

Laina handled their two patients as best she could one handed. Nick was meant to be guarding the two prisoners being escorted by ambulance, however ended up assisting her while Gary drove them to the Walk-erville hospital.

Once their duties were discharged, Gary fussed over her like a mother hen until she grew fed up and agreed to be looked over by emergency staff when they had a free moment. He was called back to the office and Laina had to admit she was grateful to see him go. She just wanted to be rid of all the attention and crawl into bed to sleep the rest of the day away.

However, unable to get in touch with her mom, she was stranded in the waiting room after the doctor had pronounced she had several bruised ribs, a badly bruised arm and should go home and rest for a few days. The fullness of what had happened threatened to overtake her, so she pushed it down and allowed sleep to come instead.

* * *

Logan approached Laina with his heart in his throat. Her head was leaning back against the wall and her eyes were closed. He crouched before her and took a moment to quietly assess the damage. Her left arm was in a sling and her neck and face had a few thin scratches that had bled, but thankfully didn't appear serious enough to leave a scar.

Logan gave her knee a gentle squeeze.

* * *

Laina roused from a light sleep and blinked owlishly into two familiar green eyes. Relief to see him hit her with force and she had to fight to keep tears at bay.

"How did you know?" she asked in a gravelly voice.

He studied her carefully, looking relieved. "Nick called. He said he couldn't get hold of your mom and that you were stranded at the ER. He wanted to take you home himself but had to stay to watch prisoners or something like that."

"Did he tell you what happened?" She hoped she would not have to relive it.

"Yeah. You are completely crazy." His voice was reasonable, but the turmoil in his eyes said that his heart was not.

Laina let her first genuine smile show through. "Apparently it was quite a spectacle."

Logan cupped her dirt-smudged cheek with a trembling hand. "Don't you scare me like that again, okay? I could have lost you."

Time was suddenly suspended as she looked into his vulnerable gaze. The bottom of Laina's world dropped out. His eyes were an open window into a depth of love he had somehow kept hidden.

"Logan Mathews, you're in love with me!" she stated in soft wonder.

Fear flickered in those green pools and he dropped his hand and looked away. He stood. "Come on, I'll take you home."

Laina was struck by his vulnerability. The last time he had let it show, they had been sixteen and she'd been in hospital with a nasty leg break and a high fever.

"You've felt that way since we were kids, haven't you?" She would not let him close off so quickly. Not when her own hope had finally come alive.

"You must be pretty sore. I hope you're planning to take the next few days off."

"Logan, look at me you big oaf." She rose stiffly from her seat.

He complied. He towered over her and was made from solid muscle, and yet Laina read fear and un-certainty in his open gaze. Her heart twisted in com-passion. Something she had buried surfaced and she smiled warmly.

Laina stepped forward and reached up on tiptoe to place a tender kiss on his cheek. She stood back and smiled into his surprised face.

"I just thought you should know the feeling is mutu-al." With that, she preceded him calmly to the red Ford pickup in the parking lot.

3

"What will happen now?" Nick asked Brian Smith.

Dressed in the typical kaki colored uniform, the African American deputy glanced at the injured man in the hospital bed beside him. Jamison Harlan had slipped into a coma shortly after his rescue from the bus wreckage.

"He's being flown to a head trauma unit in Cody. From there we just have to wait and pray he wakes up so he can tell us what he knows. I hadn't heard from him since a brief call when he was arrested with Vince a few days ago. Said he had something but needed a few extra days to lure in the big fish.

"Wish he had 'o talked then. If he had, he wouldn't be in that bed now. He was a good man. Best partner I've had yet. Smart. Real smart." He sighed deeply. "Guess now they'll have me breaking in a new one."

He looked straight at Nick, wizened brown eyes set in a weary face. The hair at his temples was sprinkled lightly with gray.

Nick stuck to the business at hand. "Anything we can do to help from our end?"

"Catch the two missing prisoners."

Nick's gaze was self-assured. "Oh we will. We've got

dogs out on their trail even as we speak. It's just a matter of time."

"When you catch Vince Moretto, call me. He's the one I'm interested in." He extended his hand and Nick shook it. "Will do. Got anything on him I should know about?"

"Just what he was convicted for, grand theft auto, but I suspect that's just the tip of the iceberg." Deputy Smith took a seat beside his partner. "I'll take over here. You catch Moretto." There was steel in his tone, suggesting this was now personal.

Nick understood. Skid marks on the bitumen suggested the bus had been run off the road by another vehicle. The driver had confirmed as much when interviewed. However, he had not been able to give a vehicle description.

"We will. I was headed out as soon as someone could take over here. I'll be in touch."

Brian nodded and his solemn gaze returned to his colleague. Nick quietly left. He would check Laina was no longer waiting around in casualty and then go join the manhunt.

* * *

Logan got into the front driver seat, put the key in the ignition and then dropped his hand to his knee and looked at his passenger. Laina was resting with her head back and her eyes closed. She looked for all the world as though nothing had happened back there. He even began doubting he'd heard her right.

* * *

Sensing she was under scrutiny, Laina's head came forward, her eyes opened and she turned to study Logan. They stared at one another for several silent minutes. Finally a small smile toyed with the edges of her lips. Logan smiled back.

"Was I imagining things in there, or did you just tell me you love me?"

A mischievous light entered Laina's clear blue eyes. "Is that what you think I said?"

Uncertainty played across Logan's features. "Did you?"

Laina grinned, loving seeing the vulnerable side to his character. "Then I guess that's what I said."

A huge smile broke across his face and he sat back and stared ahead into thin air. "Wow!"

Laina could not resist a giggle. He glanced at her again. "You really mean it?" He looked like a schoolboy who'd just been told he was free to go for summer break.

She looked into his hopeful gaze and found him adorable. "Yes, I really mean it."

Suddenly he seemed at a loss. "What happens now?"

Amusement still lurked in her expression. "We get

married tomorrow."

Logan's eyes widened in shock and Laina laughed.

"You start the car and take me home, you doof, that's what happens now."

Looking rather sheepish, Logan followed her instructions. He put the car in gear and maneuvered out of the parking lot. He was navigating traffic through central Walkerville when a wicked gleam entered his eyes.

"So, got plans for tomorrow? I know a good preacher."

Laina chuckled and pointed ahead of them. "Just take me home. I'm tired. I'll marry you next week, okay?"

Logan cast her a sideways grin. "I'm holding you to that."

Laina shook her head and got comfortable again. She had a splitting headache, a year's worth of bruising, and heavy eyelids. She would revel in their newfound relationship when she awoke from a very long nap.

* * *

The hound closest the top of the ridge let out a howl. It surged ahead, straining against its lead. Its owner, together with Nick, struggled to keep up with the excited canine. They jumped over fallen branches and wove between trees, careful of the occasional animal hole obscured by rotting vegetation.

"He's close," hunter and dog owner, Warren Beatty, stated the obvious as they topped the rise.

The dog let out several yaps and another howl and pulled hard against the lead. However, it wasn't necessary. They had found their prey.

"We've got him, Dan," Nick called back to his boss twenty yards behind them.

Dan puffed his way up the incline at a hasty walk, the best he could do after a day on a mountainside hunting down the escapee. Nick waited for his boss to reach them. He was not going down there without cover. He drew his weapon, took the safety off and checked the chambers. Good to go.

Dan reached them and drew his sidearm, gasping for breath. Nick smiled in amusement. "'Bout time you lay off the donuts, Dan."

"D'rather retire to desk duties." He panted and cut an irritated glance at his deputy.

Nick chuckled and focused on the prisoner slumped in the gully below beside a slow moving creek. His overalls were blood stained, and from this distance, he appeared to be unconscious. The crash had clearly caused serious injuries. Or it could be a trap. Nick would treat the situation as though it was the latter, although he suspected the man had simply given up.

"Cover me. I'm going down. When he's cuffed, you follow."

Dan frowned. "Who's in charge here anyway?"

Nick grinned. "You wanna tackle him in your current state?"

The sheriff rolled his eyes and waved Nick away. "Cheeky upstart."

* * *

Vince Moretto walked hunched over from Walkerville County Hospital. His cardigan smelled like mothballs, large reading glasses were perched on a hawkish latex nose, and his walking stick click-clacked with every wobbly step. Bushy eyebrows covered intense brown eyes that swept every inch of the space around him.

The getup was a roaring success. From nursing staff down to the cleaner, they had all mistook him for the old man he appeared to be. Armed with the information he needed, Vince hopped the nearest bus headed for Icy Creek. It might take several days, but he would get what he wanted. At any cost.

* * *

"We've got who we believe to be Hamish Taggart. Sorry Deputy, no sign of Vince Moretto. He seems to have just vanished into thin air," Nick informed Brian Smith over the phone from the Icy Creek sheriff's office.

Brian Smith had returned to his office in downtown Walkerville around lunchtime when Jamison Harlan had been flown to a head trauma unit further down the county.

"Does Taggart know anything that might help track Vince?"

"He says he saw someone helping Vince out of the bus after the crash but wasn't able to give a description because it was so dark. The guy apparently asked about another prisoner he wanted as well, and Vince told him he was dead. The name he used was Vaughn." Nick sat in his desk chair, phone to his ear. He kicked off his boots and peeled back soggy wet socks.

"That's Jamison's undercover ID, Vaughn Callahan."

"So we can safely say that whoever helped Vince escape, was working with them in whatever it was they were up to prior to their arrest."

"And that's what I need to know more about. What did Jamison have on Vince, and who was the bigger fish in charge of whatever that was?"

Nick was bone weary. He sighed. "I'll work on it from our end. We'd like to be kept informed if you hear anything. This thing is happening on our turf and we'd like it over with swiftly."

"Will do."

They ended the conversation there. Nick clocked off for the day and trudged to his car out back. He needed a hot shower, a long happy talk with his fiancée Emily, and a whole lot of sleep.

* * *

Logan finally walked in his front door that evening. After dropping Laina home, he had gone to work. He hadn't gotten much done with her constantly on his mind. The day had been long, but not unpleasant.

He dropped his keys on the kitchen counter and frowned at the mess his father had left behind. His car was missing from the driveway, and Logan supposed Walter had gone to visit his wife. However, the dirty dishes strewn across the counter and piled in the sink, combined with the empty beer cans littering the living room, suggested he had been home all day. So much for job hunting!

Logan's happy mood evaporated. His doubts regarding his father's conversion assailed him. He wearily collected his keys and headed out to his car, duty bound to check on his mom and his sister before he could rest for the night.

4

Laina hurriedly sorted her dirty laundry the next day, going through the pockets lest she leave a tissue in and ruin her dark clothing with fluff. She tossed the load into the washing machine. Still in the hamper was her work jacket. The sight of blood smudges was not unusual. She took it out with a sigh and repeated the pocket check. This one would need a good soaking first.

Her fingers touched a scrap of paper and she brought it out for inspection. Her brows winged upward. She had forgotten this! The blood-stained scrap of paper was folded in half. She vaguely remembered Jamison pressing it into her hand moments before their escape from the wreckage.

Sadness engulfed her. Gary had called to check on her. While they chatted, he had mentioned in passing that the prisoner she'd helped to rescue had slipped into a coma. Whether he would ever come out of it was debatable. What could he have deemed so important that he'd passed it on when he had probably known he might not make it?

Laina unfolded the note and read its brief contents. 📷☉②~⑤⑩⓪⑤~❶⑥⑤❸ʓ❺❸ʓ③②~⑨❷⓪③③~ She frowned. It was obviously a code of some kind, and printed by a computer. What did it mean? Aware this was no ordinary rescue, but that she was dealing with people who likely had things to hide, she opened her computer and scanned the message onto the hard drive. When it was saved into a folder for safe keeping, she placed the note on her kitchen counter. She would talk with Nick about it later.

She quickly went back to the laundry to complete her task. Caroline would be by any minute now to pick her up. They were going to the airport together. Laina's heart lifted. Zach was coming home.

* * *

Vince scanned the list of emergency personnel who had been present at the crash scene. Fireman Rick Wallace had been particularly helpful during that last call. He had pulled Jamison out of the bus. Alive.

A visit to the hospital earlier had confirmed that his true identity was indeed Jamison Harlan, and not Vaughn Callahan. An undercover cop! How had he managed to let that double crossing scumbag fool him? He had never been duped before. How could he have missed the signs? Had the man talked when they were arrested? Why keep his cover if he knew where the stash was?

Vince was furious. He took a deep breath and focused his anger. Jamison was out of the equation now. He needed to get it all back, or he would be next. He needed the note. The one he had caught his partner typing an hour prior to their arrest. He replayed the scene in his mind.

Vince pointed at the computer screen. "What's that about?"

Vaughn glanced over his shoulder at his partner. "You wanted plausible deniability remember?"

Vince teetered in indecision. He wanted to know. He should know. On the other hand, the risk was too great. Better Vaughn take the fall if things fell through. He understood the risks too and had volunteered for the job of temporarily hiding the stash.

"Are you sure it's safe?"

Vaughn swiveled in the desk chair in the warehouse office. His smile was enigmatic. "As safe as it'll ever be. Trust me."

Vince looked uncertainly between the coded message and his self-assured partner. He acquiesced. "Just delete that from the computer before you log off."

Vaughn hit print and then delete, turning to look at Vince with a raised brow. "Happy?"

"How will I know where it is if something happens to you?"

Vaughn's eyes narrowed dangerously. "What are you planning?"

Now it was Vince's turn to smirk. "Trust me."

Vaughn scoffed and collected the printout. He tore off the top section and folded it into his pocket. "I'll keep it on me, okay?" He attempted to preserve the *peace.*

Silence prevailed while they assessed one another.

"Fine." Vince replied coolly and strode from the office. They had a heist planned in half an hour.

Vince regretted trusting that rat. Had he truly kept that scrap of paper, or had he passed it on to the cops after their arrest? Still, to lose that cache would be certain death. If the note still existed, he had to find it. Vince glanced at the name on the bottom of the list. Rick had merely confirmed it. Laina Jackson, paramedic.

* * *

Laina hung back while Caroline hugged her youngest son at the terminal exit. The press of people either exiting the plane or coming to meet it was totally lost on all three of them. When Caroline finally stepped away, Zach spotted her and the two regarded one another with huge smiles.

"How's my big city brother?" Laina noted the dark circles under his eyes and the weariness underlying his happy expression. Yet he still looked wonderful to her.

"Looking about as good as you are. Come here and give me a hug, sis." He dropped his shoulder pack and Laina walked into his arms with a laugh.

Zach picked her up and swung her around. Laina's arm and ribs sent up sharp protests. She gasped and winced.

"Zach! Put her down!" Caroline intervened, worriedly reaching toward both of them.

"Oh sorry!" Zach set her on her feet, looking suitably chastised.

Laina's smile returned. She had missed him tremendously. It had been at least three months. "Welcome home."

Zach grinned. "Thanks. Hey, next time you wanna go jumping off wrecks and tumbling down mountains, think of me far away worrying about you and maybe play it safe? I nearly had a heart attack when Mom told me." He draped an arm around her and gently squeezed.

Laina rolled her eyes. "Oh lay off it you two. It wasn't that bad. I've just got a few bruises, that's all."

"Yeah, whatever. How should we make her pay for the gray hairs she's cost us?" Zach directed at his mother.

Caroline was beaming with pleasure to have her son with them again, even if it was for such a short time. "Oh I don't know." She pretended to think it over. "How about Laina treating us to lunch and a movie?"

Zach smiled mischievously. "Movie munchies included?"

Caroline smiled smugly at her foster daughter. "She owes us."

Laina took their banter good-naturedly. "Come on, let's grab his suitcase and get out of here. I'm starving."

Zach slung his pack on his shoulder and started to-

ward baggage collection with two of the most important women in his life by his side.

"Shall we find a really expensive restaurant?" Caroline teased.

"No!" Zach abruptly objected. "Gracie's Diner will be
fine with me."

* * *

During lunch, the usual Saturday crew arrived at
Gracie's. The private lunch for three turned into a
homecoming reunion. Logan tracked Laina down,
found Zach as well and called Wil. Nick and his fiancée Emily arrived ten minutes later. Other high school
friends joined the gang and fun-loving banter filled the
diner. Laughter was aplenty and stories were wildly
embellished. Laina loved every minute of it.

Her phone rang and interrupted her concentration
on Zach's retelling of a fishing trip gone wrong when
they were all seventeen. Still smiling, she walked outside away from the noise to answer it. She stood on
the footpath, the occasional car crawling by. Pedestri-
ans wandered the sleepy country streets at a leisurely
pace.

"Hello?"

"Laina Jackson?"

"Yes." She did not recognize the male voice.

"Oh good, I'm glad to find you. My name is Eric Finlay
and I work for the Walkerville County Police. I've been

tracking the dealings of Jamison Harlan for a while now. I'm trying to find who he was working for. But as you know, the crash this week has put my investigation on hold."

Laina listened to his sincere tone and wondered why he wanted to speak with her. "How can I help you?"

"I've been getting in touch with everyone who had contact with Mr. Harlan before he lost consciousness, and your name was on my list of people to contact. I believe he was carrying coded information that may help me and my team find the man he was working for."

Laina remembered the note she had found that morning. "Actually, I might have what you're looking for. He handed me a scrap of paper before he was pulled from the wreck. It's got a coded message on it. I only remembered it when I was doing the laundry this morning and found it in my jacket pocket."

"Hmm, would you mind if I took a look? It's imperative that we shut down the operation Jamison was involved in and it seems you might have the key to doing that."

Laina was pleased to help. "Sure. It's at home and I'm out at the moment. I'll drop it by the Icy Creek Sheriff's Office later today and you can collect it from there if you'd like?"

The voice that answered sounded satisfied. "That would be great. I'll be by the office later. Thank you for your assistance Miss Jackson."

Laina glanced back at the diner and spotted her

friends through the window laughing. "Anytime." She hung up and made a mental note to drop the note off before dinner. She strode back into the diner, eager to be part of the fun.

* * *

Laina had come in Caroline's car. As the group dispersed, Logan snagged the opportunity to have her all to himself by giving her a lift home. Zach looked exhausted and Caroline had mentioned she was hoping for a quiet night watching movies. Laina wished she could join them, but she was on an early shift the next morning and needed a good night's sleep. She knew she would stay up talking all night if she camped over.

Laina climbed into Logan's pickup and buckled her seatbelt. Already behind the wheel, Logan glanced over at her with a grin.

"That was fun. I didn't realize how much I missed the brat till now."

Knowing how well he and Zach got along, Laina just smiled in amusement. "Yeah, it's good to have him home. Even nicer to have you there to share it with."

Looking a little uncertain, Logan took a risk and leaned across the front seat to press a gentle kiss to her lips. Laina was stunned and delighted at the same time. The touch was sweet and tingled right down to her toes. It awakened a stirring of fresh love.

"You too." He pulled back and smiled.

A blush crept into her cheeks and she covered her lips with her fingertips. "I've never been kissed before," she whispered with a smile of wonder.

Laina knew Logan had spent his youth pushing girls away for fear of rejection.

"Me either." He cupped her cheek with a work roughened hand.

They held each other's gaze, reveling in the delight of discovering each other. Logan was tempted to go back for seconds. Laina read it in his eyes and her smile widened.

"I think you should drive me home now, and maybe don't do that again till we're married. I like it too much."

Although clearly disappointed, Logan acquiesced. "Fair enough, Ace. Those lips of yours are tempting. So, is our wedding still on for next week?"

"Sure, I just need a dress. Now let's go."

Logan chuckled and started the engine. In truth, neither one felt the need to rush. Courtship was wonderfully enjoyable.

* * *

A surge of anger flared dangerously to life as he watched the couple in the car from a safe distance. She would pay. The anger helped him focus, making his intent unstoppable. First he would start with the message, then her. It was only fair. His life was close to being in ruins. He had to rectify it and this was the only way he could see to do it.

5

Laina unlocked her front door to the sound of Logan's truck backing out of the driveway. She flicked the light switch by the door. She kicked off her shoes and strolled across the main living area of her small country cottage, passing the red sofa and then the dark wooden dining table and chairs.

The kitchen overlooked the open space from the far wall. She placed her purse on the dark marble counter and circled it to open the refrigerator against the wall. She was reaching for the orange juice when a floorboard in the hallway creaked.

Laina closed the door and turned around. The house was relatively old and the internal framework and roof tended to groan with heat expansion and contraction. However, the floor had needed a complete overhaul when she bought the house, and now creaked only occasionally under the weight of a person. The hallway was to the right of the kitchen, leading to the back of the house. There were two bedrooms, a laundry and a bathroom.

Laina's eyes swept the room. Her now keen gaze noted dusty footprints beyond the counter, heading toward the hallway. One glance told her the shoe size was much bigger than hers, and Logan had not been in her house since she last mopped. Only Caroline had.

Besides her purse and keys, the counter was empty. Hadn't she sat the note on the bench that morning? Had she left it in her bedroom? She began doubting herself. No, it had been on the counter. She was sure of it. She drew her phone from her pocket and dialed Logan's number while at the same time reaching for the heavy-base skillet in the dish rack.

Logan picked up on the other end with a cheerful tone. "Hi Ace."

Another floorboard creaked, this time closer to the kitchen entrance.

"Someone's in my house!" she whispered and crouched behind the counter.

"You're too quiet. What was that again?"

Laina dared not say a word. She could hear the soft footfalls now on the other side of the bench. She gently sat her phone on the floor beside her and gripped the handle with both hands. Her knuckles whitened and her pulse pounded in her ears.

Closer, closer. They stopped. Whoever was there stood only inches away from discovering her.

Adrenaline charged through her veins. Laina rose up and swung the pan with a vengeance. An arm came up to shield the intruder's face, taking the brunt of the impact. The man let out a yelp of pain and stumbled backward. She could see him now. A black balaclava covered his face, showing only two menacing brown eyes that suddenly locked onto her. He recovered quickly, and charged toward her.

Fight or flight? Laina drew back the pan and swung it with all her might. He dodged and caught the skillet, wrenching it from her hands. Split seconds later, he rammed her into the refrigerator. His forearm pressed against her collarbone and pinned her against the fridge door. He used the handle of the pan against her neck to cut off air circulation.

Fear and panic fueled a desperate move to free herself. Laina scratched at his face through the balaclava. The ploy worked. He growled with anger and his grip weakened. She took the opportunity to knee him in the groin. He howled with pain and she broke loose.

Laina made a dash for the front door. Her hand was reaching for the knob when a stronger one reefed her backward by her shirt collar. Her terrified scream was cut short as she landed on her back next to the sofa. Her sore arm sent up protests, as did the hip that took the brunt of the fall. She saw him then. He leaned over her and dark eyes sparked fury. His lips curled into a snarl.

"You're going to die for that."

Where she should have felt fear, Laina was suddenly incensed. He dared to come into her home, attack her and think he had a right to take her life when she defended herself. Her face hardened. She struck upward with the palm of her hand, finding her mark well.

Her attacker roared, stumbled back and clutched his broken nose. Laina scrambled to her feet and grabbed a chunky snow globe from the small table beside the sofa. She launched it at his head ruthlessly and, not waiting to see if she hit him, turned to grab the glass lamp from the table also. A fist connected with the side of her head as she was reaching.

The force sent her crashing into the table. The lamp toppled to the floor and shattered. Stunned by the blow, Laina's legs gave out and she landed with a thud beside it. Spots danced before her eyes and she lost her bearings. The toe of a boot came from seemingly nowhere and found her stomach with brutal accuracy. All oxygen left her body and she doubled over on the floor, unable to fight back.

Lights flashed across the living room window, signaling someone had pulled into her driveway. Footsteps inside the cottage retreated and the backdoor slammed shut. Laina was unable to move for the excruciating pain in her midsection.

"Laina!" Logan's petrified voice reached her dull senses.

The front door burst open to the sound of car tires screeching on the street behind her house.

"Laina!" Logan called again, and then spotted her on the floor by the sofa. He dropped to his knees by her side and looked into her agonized face.

She managed to draw a breath. "Logan, watch – out - he's-"

"Sh, he's gone. A car just took off out the back. Are you okay?" He gently brushed blond locks of hair from her face. Logan looked ill with worry.

Laina concentrated on breathing and was relieved to

find it returning to normal. She raised herself up on her right elbow and Logan helped her sit. The world was spinning. She clutched her stomach with her left hand to help ease the pain and grabbed a fist full of Logan's shirt with her right.

"You came." Tears unexpectedly spilled onto her lashes and she finally met his gaze.

Logan swallowed hard and his eyes looked a little moist. "I heard yelling over the phone and turned my car around."

"What if he comes back?" She could not fight any longer. She was helpless and it scared her. Despite her best efforts, her attacker had overpowered her. "He said he was going to kill me."

Logan's gaze hardened and the muscles in his jaw worked angrily. "I hope he does come back. I'll give him a taste of his own medicine."

Laina caught the challenge in his tone and found some comfort. She was safe for now. No one in their right mind would mess with Logan or those he loved.

He turned his attention to first aid. "Where are you hurt?"

"He kicked me in the stomach."

"Anything feel broken?" He stood so that he could help her to her feet.

"No. I got hit in the head. It hurts and I'm dizzy." Laina clutched his arm and tried to stand. The dizziness hit full force and she just couldn't manage it.

Alarm entered his gaze. She'd told him enough about head injuries to know this could be serious.

"I'm calling an ambulance."

"No!" Laina desperately needed to be somewhere that felt safe. "Take me to Mom's."

"I know she's a good nurse an' all, but she's no doctor. You should get a head scan." He slipped an arm around her waist to keep her upright, for which she was grateful. She was beginning to shake.

"Please?" Laina's voice broke, much to her chagrin. "Let's go to Mom's." She knew most people thought Logan was tough, but when it came to tears, he had never been able to find it in his heart to argue.

"Okay." He gently lifted her. "We'll call the sheriff from the car. Let's hope Wil's uncle Dan can catch this guy. 'Cos if he doesn't, I will, and when I get my hands on him..." Logan left the sentence hang, as he kicked the door open wider and carried Laina to his truck.

As soon as she was safely tucked in the cab, he whipped out his cell and dialed. He climbed in on his side just as the phone picked up on the other end. One glance at Laina and he hastily gunned the engine and talked while he steered the vehicle to Caroline's place.

* * *

Caroline opened the front door and all color drained from her face. "What happened?"

Logan brushed by her and carried Laina through to the kitchen. She was still holding her head. Caroline followed.

"Someone broke into her house and attacked her. She called me just before it happened and I came as quick as I could. The guy was intending to kill her but did a runner when I got there."

"I can walk you know," Laina's dry tone interrupted.

Logan ignored her mild protest and gently sat her on a chair at the kitchen table. She knew he would not be satisfied until Caroline looked her over and pronounced a clean bill of health.

"Someone what?" Caroline knelt before her only daughter. She shifted her gaze from Logan's anxious face to Laina's. "Tell me what happened."

"Just what Logan said. The guy was waiting for me in my house, and he took the note." The shakes had left and her equilibrium was returning.

Logan frowned. "What note?"

Laina met his gaze and held it. "The coded message a prisoner gave me the morning of the bus crash. The same message I got a call about this afternoon."

The implications of what she was saying began to register. This was bigger than just a break in. It was a planned hit.

"I'm going to talk to Nick." Logan drew his phone from his jeans pocket and perched on a stool at the kitchen counter to make the call. Caroline focused on Laina.

"Tell me where you're hurt."

Zach entered the room from the hallway, obviously having heard voices. "What's going on?"

Caroline began running her hands along limbs checking for breaks or bleeding. "Someone attacked Laina."

"What?" Zach's exclamation matched his mother's. "Who?"

"We don't know. It was a break in. Logan's talking to Nick about it now." Caroline checked pupil dilation and then the place Laina had been holding. There was a decent sized egg beneath the skin. She gently probed Laina's midsection and other than wincing in discomfort, she did not cry out. Her color was returning which was a positive sign. There seemed to be no internal bleeding.

Zach looked to Logan for answers. Logan acknowledged him with a distracted wave as he conversed with Nick.

"You okay?" He laid a hand on her shoulder.

Laina mustered a smile to reassure him and then focused on flexing her bruised arm. "I'll be fine. It's not like I haven't been hit before."

The casual remark froze Caroline in place. She must have forgotten Laina's tough few years with her uncle before she and Zach had taken her in. The reminder had to be painful. Caroline exchanged a glance with Zach. Laina noticed, but was too tired to address the undercurrent in the room. She propped her aching head on her hand and leant on the table.

"Can I have an aspirin?"

"Of course," Caroline replied softly, clearly emotionally shaken. She got up to fetch one from the cupboard above the bench. Laina suspected she was taking her time in order to school her features and calm her heart.

"Thanks Nick. Yeah, see you soon." Logan disconnected the line and dropped his phone on the counter. "Nick's coming. He's stopping by your place first to take a look and chat with Dan Fisher, then he'll be here to get your statement. He said he might know a bit of what this is all about."

"And the scumbag that did this?" Zach asked pointedly, his outrage also evident.

Logan looked none too pleased. "He got away, for now."

Zach shook his head and bent down to hug Laina from the side. Laina was touched by his kindness and tears blurred her vision. She clutched his arm gently resting against her collar bone and remembered the terrifying sensation of being choked. An involuntary shudder shook her frame.

Zach must have felt her tense. "Don't worry, Laina. If he comes back, I'll strangle him with my bare hands."

"Get in line," Logan replied flatly.

Laina wiped her eyes and chuckled. As miserable as she felt right now, it was good to know she was cared about. She took the glass of water and swallowed the pills Caroline offered. Meanwhile Caroline pressed a cold cloth gently against the swelling in her skull. It was looking to be a long night.

6

It was late when Nick finally departed, leaving them all with a clearer picture of events. Unable to sleep, Zach suggested a movie and popcorn. Caroline was glad for the idea, determined to monitor Laina's head injury. Laina seemed eager to avoid the strong possibility of bad dreams.

"Are you staying?" she asked Logan as he rose from his seat at the kitchen table.

Logan must have caught the hopeful gleam in her eyes, but at the same time seemed hesitant to trespass upon Caroline's hospitality. Zach read his pause and restrained a mischievous smile. He wanted to see more interaction between his friend and his sister. Something had definitely changed between them since the last time he had visited.

"Stay Logan," he invited with merry eyes. "You can pick the movie."

Laina rolled her eyes. "That's just what I need after what happened tonight." She rose stiffly from the table where they had all been talking over cups of coffee. "More fuel for nightmares."

Logan indulged her with an amused smile. "How about a western?"

Laina appeared satisfied. "Good. I've had enough action to last me a lifetime."

"I'll say!" Caroline gathered the empty mugs. She took them to the sink and dug through the cupboard for some microwave popcorn.

"You guys go ahead and set everything up while I help Mom," Zach suggested.

"Okay." Laina wearily scuffed toward the den just off the front entrance with Logan a protective step behind her.

Caroline snatched Zach by the shirtsleeve and tugged him over to the corner of the kitchen near the kettle. Zach was surprised by the rough action and laughed at her conspiratorial expression. His mother quickly clamped a hand over his mouth.

"Sh!" She glanced at the empty doorway the pair had just passed through and met her son's amused gaze. She removed her hand. "Is it just me, or is something going on between those two?"

Zach grinned. "You noticed it too huh?"

Caroline looked thoughtful. Zach mentally reviewed Logan's uncharacteristic attentiveness to his sister. His protective streak had always run a mile wide. However, he seemed to suddenly feel free to show the tender side of his nature toward her.

Zach studied his mother's pensive expression and couldn't help a wicked grin. "It's been a long time coming, don't you think?"

A slow smile spread across Caroline's lips. "Amen to that. Grab the ice cream."

Zach chuckled and did as he was told.

＊　＊　＊

"You called in sick tomorrow, right?"

Laina punched the sofa pillow and tried to get comfortable. "Mom made the call. Nate was apparently livid about the break in."

She had first met her boss when he worked her position ten years ago. He had rescued her after she'd had a nasty fall from a helicopter. Since then he had slowly worked his way up to being in charge of the rescue paramedic division in Walkerville.

"He's not the only one." Logan watched her struggle to find the right position on her half on the sofa with her bruised arm and sore head. "Here." He took the pillow from her and placed it on his lap. "Stretch out and be comfortable."

Laina's cheeks turned a nice shade of pink and she smiled at him warmly. Logan's eyes twinkled with amusement as he held her gaze, becoming aware of her shy side. He reveled in the knowledge she was officially his girl and he was free to show it. It was clear she was still adjusting to that freedom as well.

He knew they would have to face a thousand excited questions from family and friends regarding the two of them sooner or later. He was tempted to taunt them a little first by making them wait and wonder. Yet the idea of snuggling her close was too enticing. She must have felt the same way, for she grinned and stretched out on her good side on the sofa with her head on the pillow in his lap. Logan gently ran his fingers through her long blond hair and slowly the tension of the day melted away.

"That's nice." Her eyelids drooped shut.

Logan smiled to himself. It sure was. "Your hair is soft and it smells real good."

Laina smiled in contentment and sleep crowded in. Caroline and Zach wandered in bearing bowls of ice cream and bags of popcorn to share. They both noticed the couple on the couch and exchanged smiling glances. Zach noted his sister drifting off to sleep and seemed pleased she was getting some rest.

"What are we watching?" he whispered.

Logan aimed the remote at the DVD player and scrolled through the disc menu.

"'The Big Country' with Gregory Peck." He pressed play.

Caroline dropped into her favorite armchair and pulled her knees up, a bag of popcorn in her hands. "Oh goodie. That's one of my favorites."

Logan couldn't help but smile. Sometimes she was like an overgrown kid. He wished his own mother could let down her guard and learn to have fun like that. He only hoped she was safe tonight. How had her evening gone with his dad?

Zach stretched out in the other armchair, his feet on a large yellow fluffy footstool. "This is new, Mom. When did you get it?"

Caroline grinned. "A friend from my Bible group gave it to me for my birthday. She said it reminded her of my sunny personality."

Zach snorted. "You think?"

Caroline tossed a handful of popcorn at him and he laughed. The movie started and conversation died down. Somewhere between feuding clans and a happy ending, Caroline also dropped off to sleep. Zach covered her with a rug and changed DVDs.

"So," he casually asked as he got comfortable in his chair again, "how long have you two been seeing each other?"

Logan was acutely aware of their past. Ten years ago they had both vied for Laina's attention. "About twenty-four hours. Be honest with me, Zach, does it bother you?"

Zach met his friend's serious gaze and restrained a laugh. "Are you kidding? She's my sister."

"Not by blood and we both know it," Logan returned calmly.

There was a short silence while they assessed one another.

"She's all yours, trust me. You can have her crazy bent for adventure and all her big words. Her snoring is all yours too."

Logan relaxed imperceptibly. He had his friend's blessing and it meant the world to him. "I'll take it all with pleasure."

Zach leveled him with a pointed look. "Just don't ever hurt her or I'll break your neck."

"Easiest promise I ever made." Logan's smile was relaxed. His expression became thoughtful. "Hey, Laina mentioned you've got a girl back in New York. How's that going?"

Zach's happy mood slipped away. "I don't know. I'm confused. Brylie's complicated."

Logan's lips pulled up at one corner. "You got yourself one of those hey?"

Zach passed him an amused smile. "Apparently."

Logan shoved aside all humor and drove straight to the heart of the matter. He knew Zach expected nothing less than candor. "Is she the one God's got for you or are you marking time?"

"I'm not sure anymore. I thought God was in it, but lately she's more interested in career advancement than in our relationship. Going to church together has dropped off too. I'm finding myself working longer hours, and because I'm so tired, I'm slipping out of good habits like Bible reading and prayer. It's weird. I've got everything by the world's standards; a good job with a promising future, a beautiful girl, a nice apartment and a great car, but it all seems so hollow. Am I just being discontent, or somewhere along the line have I strayed from the path God had planned?"

Logan's brows rose and he exhaled slowly. "Tough question. Maybe time away from it all will help give you a clearer perspective?"

Zach sighed. "I hope so. How about you?"

Logan's smile was contentment itself. "Never been happier. I've got a job that's downright freezing in winter and boiling in summer, a rundown rental house I'm sharing with my dad, but on the whole, made sweeter every day by a really great girl."

Zach chuckled and pressed play with the remote.

"Seriously, though, I'll be praying you find the right way to go."

Zach looked grateful. "Thanks."

They settled in to watch the next movie, an action thriller.

* * *

Laina wearily dropped into the roller chair at the computer desk in her old room. It had been converted into a study when she'd bought her house and moved out a couple of years ago.

She turned on the computer and rubbed tired, scratchy eyes. She could hear movement and voices in the kitchen as Caroline and the boys had breakfast. It was Sunday and they were all planning to go to church together. She occasionally had to work Sundays due to shift work, and although she'd taken the day as sick leave, found it difficult to just walk away when she knew she was rostered on.

She opened her e-mail and began sorting through the new mail in her inbox. Her roster, good. A get well message from her boss, Nate. Another from Gary. A notice about upcoming training days.

Laina's mouse paused over one from an old high

school address of Logan's. She frowned. Logan was not into e-mail and didn't even own a computer. The message was dated today. She mentally shrugged and clicked on open. Her eyes scanned the short missive and her blood ran cold.

'I saw you. I know where you live and I'll be paying you a visit.'

This was not the voice of her beloved. She realized with sickening clarity that it had to be from her attacker. Did he still have her under surveillance?

Violent flashbacks from last night flooded her vision and fear slammed into her like a bus. Burning rage bubbled dangerously to the surface.

Laina bolted from the room and fled to the backyard.

7

All three heads in the kitchen swiveled toward the back of the house when they heard screaming.

With a puzzled expression, Caroline sat her coffee cup on the counter. "That sounds like Laina."

Fear and adrenaline jolted Logan and he sprang from his seat at the table and sprinted for the back exit. Zach was close behind on his heels. They burst out the door onto the porch and came to an abrupt halt with what they saw.

"What in the world?" Zach looked relieved and confused.

Caroline stumbled over the doorjamb, her eyes wide with astonishment at her daughter screaming in apparent rage. They watched Laina in stunned silence as she wildly took to anything in her reach with a broom. Logan exhaled with relief.

"I've got choices! I've got choices! I've got choices!" Laina screamed at the top of her lungs, angrily hurling the broom over the back fence.

Logan recognized immediately what was happening. He had been there many times himself. Caroline covered her mouth with trembling fingers. None of them had ever seen her react this way. The closest to this kind of anger was the day she awoke in hospital after having been kidnapped and seriously injured. She had thrashed in bed trying to escape while Caroline and Zach physically restrained her. Back then it had been due to repressed memories of losing her father in a car accident when she was thirteen.

Zach's brows were furrowed with worry and he stepped off the porch, heading toward his sister. Logan laid a restraining hand on his arm.

"Wait, Zach. I think I know what's going on."

Zach looked into his friend's grim expression. He reluctantly nodded. Logan approached the wild woman kicking the picket fence.

She must have heard his footsteps, because she spun to face him, clearly ready to fight. Logan instinctively prepared to block any blows.

He understood the fear in her eyes. It took her a moment to register that it was him facing her and not an attacker.

Seconds ticked by. She sucked in air, seemingly unaware she had been holding her breath. The fear did not leave her and anger barked hot on its heels. Painful reality appeared to wash over her as she held his determined gaze.

"I have choices!" she hurled the words at him.

He stopped only a few feet from her. "Yeah, and he took them from you!"

"How dare he!"

"He doesn't have the right!"

"It's *my* house! He wants to kill me in *my* house!"

Laina spun to kick at the fence again.

Logan did not miss the use of present tense in her phrasing. He injected challenge into his tone to draw the last of her anger out.

"What are you going to do about it?"

He could see her fury waning. Each kick had less and less force.

Defeat suddenly dropped over her like a suffocating blanket and gut-wrenching sobs broke from her chest. Her hands fell to her sides and her shoulders slumped.

He hated the extreme approach, but having gone through violent episodes himself, he understood Laina needed to fully vent her feelings if any kind of healing was to take place.

"I'm not strong enough."

Logan's heart twisted painfully. He empathized with her feelings of helplessness. He closed the short distance between them and wrapped his arms around her gently from behind. Laina flinched and then surrendered. She could not control the sobs of brokenness.

He supposed the present violence from her attacker had opened a wound that had not quite healed. True, she had forgiven her uncle. But the feelings of fear from another's hatred were just as real now as when she was a teenager. He hoped the safety of his arms would provide a measure of comfort. It must have, for she turned in his embrace and allowed herself to be enfolded.

"You're right," he replied softly, his chin resting upon her head, "you're not strong enough. But you don't have to be. You're not facing this guy alone. It's not like when you were a kid, Laina."

Logan's calm assurance must have brought a huge sense of relief, as she sighed deeply. He knew then that he had read her accurately and offered the one thing she was subconsciously seeking: protection.

"He's been watching me." She drew in gulps of air even as the crying subsided.

Logan cupped her face with large calloused hands and looked steadfastly into her anxious gaze. "I'm not leaving you alone for a moment." Reading the flicker of doubt in her eyes, he quickly countered it. "And when I can't be there, Zach will be. Do you understand? This guy is not going to get at you again."

Laina nodded, visibly forcing her breathing back under control. Logan held her a little while longer. He let go only when he felt her muscles relax under his touch.

She seemed to come to her senses. The sight of the broom on the grass over the back fence, and the bedraggled roses brought a large dose of shame to her red-rimmed eyes.

"I'm so sorry!" She started to cry all over again. "The roses... the fence..."

Logan chuckled and moved enough to look into her face. "Remind me in the future to hide the broom whenever I make you mad."

His humor brought an unexpected smile to her face and she wiped at her tears with a sleeve. He draped his arm around her shoulders and steered her toward the house. She spotted Caroline and Zach sitting patiently on the back step and looked guilty for her outburst.

"I'm sorry Mom. Sorry Zach." She sniffed and bit her lower lip.

"There's plenty of grace for us all, sweetie." Caroline rose with arms extended.

Laina walked into them.

Zach shook his head incredulously at Logan. "Have you got a death wish? I'd have approached her only with a ten foot pole!"

Laina laughed softly and stepped away from her mom, wiping the last of her tears with a shaky hand. Logan tussled her hair playfully.

"Nah, she looks tough, but on the inside she's just a big pussy cat."

Laina smiled at him, obviously still too shaken to give a good comeback.

"So." Zach leveled her with a serious look. "What got you going?"

Laina sighed. "An e-mail."

Zach arched an eyebrow. "An e-mail set you off like a fourth of July cracker?"

Laina gave him a shove.

"Must have been some e-mail," Caroline remarked with a concerned frown.

"It was. Go see for yourselves." Laina gestured to the house.

"We will, don't you worry about that," Caroline assured, clearly determined to address whatever had upset her.

Zach preceded them into the house and led the precession to the study. Logan draped a protective arm around Laina's shoulders and they followed.

* * *

"So this guy has hacked into my old e-mail address and used it to stalk Laina?" Logan summed up the situation.

"Yeah, I've had it happen to me before," Zach answered distractedly as he tapped away at the computer keys. He glanced over his shoulder at his sister and his friend. "Not being stalked."

Caroline was pacing near the doorway, phone to her ear. Zach had asked her to talk to the e-mail service provider's support team, while he tried other means of tracking the origin of the message.

"Someone hacked into my account and sent a scam e-mail supposedly from me to everyone on my contact list. The message said I was stranded at a foreign airport and my wallet had been stolen. It was asking for money. I found out the day it happened because my phone didn't stop ringing. Everyone I knew was calling me to see if I was okay and needed help."

Laina's memory of that incident jogged and she smiled. "Yeah, I remember that."

Zach tossed an amused smile at her over his shoulder. "So do I. You were the first call I got. You gave me the third degree for not being safety conscious and then for going overseas without telling you."

Logan's tone was dry. "Sounds about right."

Laina jabbed him in the ribs playfully. His twinkling eyes met hers. "Be careful. Two can play at that game."

"The thing is, even though the message is sent from another e-mail account, every computer has a distinct IP address. If I can trace the IP address, we can find the location the message was sent from," Zach explained.

Logan exhaled impatiently. "Why's it taking so long?"

Zach continued working. "Whoever sent this knew they might be traced and they've covered their tracks well."

"So you can't find where it was sent from?" A spike of fear elevated Laina's adrenaline. If they couldn't find this guy, he would come for her again.

Zach kept tapping away at the keys on the keyboard. Screen after screen popped up and disappeared. He had long ago delved into a world Laina did not understand.

"Oh I can find it. I just need this guy to go online again. Why don't you two visit Nick? He mentioned last night he wanted to see the copy of the note you were given by that prisoner. Make sure you tell him about this latest development. I'll handle things here."

Logan shook his head. "No dude. You're coming with us. There's no way I'll be able to explain what it is you're doing here." He waved his hand at the screen with a frown.

Zach stopped and stared at him. "You've got to be kidding."

"I want you to catch this guy as much as everyone

else here, probably more," Laina entered the debate, "but you're not going to find him if his computer is off, right?"

Zach sighed. "Yeah. At least let me identify his IP address before we go. Give me an hour."

Logan raked a hand through his hair. He clearly wanted action, and having to sit around and wait appeared to be pure torture. Yet the chances of nailing this guy were higher if they knew where he had gone to ground. "Okay. An hour."

Laina mentally sagged with relief.

"Let's just hope he didn't use an internet café or the local library," Logan muttered.

Zach glanced at him in surprise. That possibility obviously hadn't entered his calculations. Logan noticed and smiled.

"See, you need a detective like me on the case."

Zach rolled his eyes and went back to work. Laina shook her head.

* * *

Laina stood in the center of her living room two hours later and a shudder ran through her. She felt chilled to the bone. The temperature was warm; nevertheless, she rubbed her arms and hugged herself.

The crime scene technicians had been through, evidenced by the fine film of white dust covering every surface where fingerprints had been taken. Nick, Zach and Logan were discussing the evidence that had been collected and analyzed so far.

Several drops of blood near the sofa indicated that she had indeed inflicted some serious pain to her attacker's nose. She wasn't sure what to make of her satisfaction in that knowledge.

She had been through so much in her past and had forgiven those who had hurt and abused her, and she wanted to be able to do that again. However, as her mind replayed the violence from that night, she had to admit that forgiveness was far from her at this point.

"You're sure it was him?" she heard Zach ask Nick.

"Positive." Nick pointed. "DNA tests from the blood there matched those on the database. Vince Morretto is Laina's attacker. And you say you found the IP address for the person who sent her the e-mail?"

Zach studied the obvious signs of a struggle and answered distractedly. "Yeah. He didn't go online, so I couldn't find his location."

"No matter." Nick shrugged it off. "The cyber crime unit can handle that. Those guys live for that stuff. Hey Laina," he drew her attention and diverted the discussion, "can we see the copy of that code you mentioned?"

Laina's head came up from staring at the blood on the floor and her gaze locked with Nick's. She mentally shook off the image and tried to focus on what he was asking. "Sure."

She crossed woodenly to the large oak desk against the far wall and turned her computer on. In minutes she had the scanned image on the screen and was printing out several copies.

Each of the men took a copy, studying it quietly. Zach frowned, glanced at the computer and then at Laina.

"It can't be that simple!"

"What are you thinking?" Nick puzzled.

"Jump up for a second, sis'?" Zach took Laina's seat at the desk as soon as she vacated it.

The three watched him curiously as he opened Microsoft Word and began tapping out the alphabet. He then followed it with numbers one through to ten. He highlighted the text, copied and pasted it and then changed the font of the second set of letters and numbers several times until he found a match. He leaned back in his chair.

"Wingdings two, my friends."

Logan looked stunned. "Are you serious? That's way too easy!"

"For a sophisticated operator, you'd think Jamison could come up with something better," Nick muttered.

"Yeah, but think about it guys," Laina pointed out, "he had to make something fast and simple that the department could crack without an established key to help break the code. And for the average person, it's not that easy to figure out."

Logan shrugged. His look said that he would have chosen something nobody could break. Zach began matching symbols with the code key. Finally he sat back and they all stared at one line of crucial information.

'98kensingtonwaywalkerville.'

"Do you suppose that's where they hid the loot?" Logan wondered aloud.

"That's assuming Vince has been stealing cash or jewels," Nick pointed out. "For all we know, it may be drugs."

"Or antiquities," Zach added.

Everyone looked at him as though he'd lost his mind.

He held his hands up in defense. "Hey, people do that. Antiques are worth a fortune on the black market."

"So are secrets."

Logan glanced at Laina sideways in surprise and ruffled her hair. "Good thinking, Ace. I knew there was a reason we brought you along."

"You mean other than for my stunning good looks?"

Logan's eyes lit with an appreciative gleam and travelled from her head to her toes and back again. Laina blushed under his warm scrutiny.

"That too."

"Alright guys, let's hit the road." Nick was all business. "There's only one way to find out what's at that address, and it won't happen while we're standing here guessing."

8

"Why are you just telling me this now?" Laina scolded Logan mildly as they rode along in his truck behind Nick and Sheriff Dan in the squad car.

After a stop at their office to find details on the information they had decoded, and having established it was a residential address, Nick arranged a warrant to search the premises. Deputy Brian Smith was meeting them there, also eager to see what Vince Moretto was willing to risk coming back for.

"You had bigger fish to fry and the time never seemed to be right," Logan defended his silence.

Zach took in the exchange from his seat against the window and barely smothered a smile. "You two sound like an old married couple."

Laina was sandwiched between them in the middle and was none too pleased about being left in the dark. She ignored her brother momentarily.

"Just for your information, Logan Mathews, you are important to me and so is whatever's happening in your life."

Logan could not restrain a chuffed smile. "Oh wow, that's really nice."

Laina scowled. "Don't get all cute with me."

Logan's eyes lit with a hopeful gleam. "You think I'm cute?"

Laina huffed with impatience. "Stop deflecting my anger! I'm trying to reprimand you for not telling me your father's back in town, and *living* with you no less!"

Logan stared at the road and frowned. "She hasn't changed a bit since you left, Zach. She still uses big words all the time."

Zach stifled a laugh. "I could have told you that. I still get an earful over the phone on a regular basis."

Laina was outraged. "Am I the only one concerned that Logan's formally abusive father has returned?"

Logan turned onto a residential street and Zach began reading house numbers.

"Don't get me wrong, Ace," Logan explained as he pulled to the curb behind the squad car several houses down from number ninety-eight. "I ain't happy he's back and I don't think he's changed all that much, despite his claim he's met Jesus. But I'm a big boy. He can't hurt me anymore."

Logan switched off the engine.

"And your mom and Tia?"

Logan sighed. "Yeah that bothers me."

He got out of the car and they followed.

"I've been around Mom's place every spare minute I can get. Things are quiet for now and I'm hoping it stays that way. If it doesn't, I'll file assault charges so fast Dad'll wonder what hit him."

Laina sympathized. She supposed there wasn't anything else he could do. She had been blessed in regard to her uncle Rylan's conversion ten years ago. It had been genuine, and the way he treated her had changed. He now had a feisty wife, Jade, whom he had met at church a couple of years ago. Logan's Dad, on the other hand, was an unknown entity. Only time would tell if his confession of faith was serious. Laina only hoped no one got hurt in the interim.

In front of them, Nick and Dan conferred on the pavement with Deputy Brian Smith, who had been parked and waiting. Logan didn't appear worried about Nick's reaction to sticking his nose into police affairs. He sidled up to them and listened in. Laina was a little more reticent, and hung back at the truck with Zach.

* * *

"Are you sure there's no need for another squad car?" Nick asked Deputy Smith.

"I wouldn't think so. After talking with you on the phone, I checked with city council records. This place is owned by a Mrs. Miranda Wilcox. She's deceased and the lawyer handling the will was free to tell us the home is only days away from finalization."

"Who did it go to?" Dan asked curiously.

"My partner, Jamison Harlan."

"Not surprising," Nick remarked. "The house being empty means whatever's here would remain untouched. And with it still officially in his aunt's name, and him using an undercover title, no one he was working with would think to monitor it."

Brian nodded toward the small two-bedroom bunga-low several houses down. "I'll take the front door with Dan, and Nick, you cover the back entrance."

Logan did not miss the fact he was ignored, but nei-ther did he take it personally. When the group split up, he followed his friend.

"Logan, I know you've got a personal interest in this case." Nick strode to the side yard. "But you can't just tag along on a search." Nick stopped at a waist high wooden fence.

"I get the whole police business thing." Logan put a hand for support and then a foot up on the top of the fence and made a smooth leap. "I won't touch anything or disturb any evidence, and I won't get in your way."

"That's reassuring," Nick remarked dryly and deftly scaled the rickety structure. "I was thinking more along the lines of you being unarmed and untrained."

They faced one another. "The deputy says it's not likely anyone's here."

Nick hesitated. "Still..."

Logan shrugged. "You take the lead. I'm just here to watch your back."

Nick rolled his eyes heavenward and he drew his weapon. Nothing had changed since they were kids. A small smile toyed with his lips as he carefully edged along the side wall and peered into the yard. Empty, and very unkempt.

He cautiously approached the back door. He was on the porch reaching for the door, only to have it fly open, missing his face by a matter of inches.

Nick dodged and stumbled back into a wooden rock-er, offsetting his balance. Two young men wearing bala-clavas charged out, heading for the side of the house. Logan tackled the nearest one without thought and brought him to the ground with a thud. Nick recovered and ran after the other.

"Stop, police!" he shouted the warning as they rounded the house.

The man spun and raised his right arm, and it was then Nick saw the weapon in his hand.

* * *

Laina heard the gunshot and pushed away from her relaxed position against the truck. Her pulse acceler-ated. It had come from either in, or behind the house. Logan. Nick.

Zach dropped from his perch on the hood of the vehicle, his intent gaze on the empty front yard. Yell-ing came from within the house and footsteps echoed even from this distance. Dan Fisher tore open the front door and trotted down the stairs. Zach seemed to de-bate whether to go and help, then took one glance at Laina's ashen face and must have decided she needed him more.

Someone in a balaclava sprinted across the yard and then the road toward a blue sports car. He was only a matter of thirty yards away.

Dan fired several shots and the man stopped with his car door open to return fire. His movements, although rushed, were calculated. And so was his aim. Dan dropped to the ground with a groan, clutching his midsection.

Suddenly the gunman swung his raised arm to the onlookers. Zach dove for cover behind the truck, taking Laina down with him as three short, sharp shots rang out. Laina and Zach hit the grass beside the truck with Zach landing on top of her. An engine revved, two more shots toward the house followed, and tires screeched.

The gunman was gone. As the sound of raised voices and urgent shouts ensued, it became obvious to Laina that the sense of dread in her gut was warranted. He had left destruction in his path.

* * *

"Have you got him?" Brian swept past Logan who had the first assailant pinned to the ground with an arm twisted behind his back, and his right cheek pressed into the grass. There was a handgun that had been wrested free lying a short distance away near a bed of neglected roses.

"He ain't goin' nowhere." All of Logan's strength concentrated on holding the man angrily cursing and writhing under his brutal grip. "Where's Nick?"

"Just keep him there while I secure the area," Brian ordered tersely.

Logan gritted his teeth. "Piece of cake," he muttered sarcastically. "I could go a cup of tea while I'm at it. Could someone just cuff this guy?"

His testy request was ignored as the deputy disappeared around the corner of the house.

"Let me up!" the assailant demanded hotly, his face mottled with rage.

Logan glanced at the man who had gone for his gun when he was tackled. "Like that's gonna happen anytime soon."

The struggle had been fierce, but a solid left blow to the man's jaw had rendered him momentarily stunned. Long enough for Logan to get the gun and acquire a better hold.

Logan's worried gaze lifted to the side of the house where he wished he could follow. Was Nick okay? And what about Zach and Laina? He had no choice but to stay put and wait for reinforcement.

* * *

Zach's weight rolled off her and Laina sat up. From where she was, she could see Nick crouched beside Sheriff Dan. Her first instinct was to stay out of sight in case more shots were fired, however her training kicked in.

She rose stiffly to her feet, about to run to his aid when Zach's labored breathing caught her attention. She glanced down at where he still lay, face twisted in agony, jaw clenched to prevent screaming out in pain. Shock hit her like a mule kick to her chest. Her brother had been shot.

9

Laina dropped to Zach's side, unzipped his jacket and lifted his blood-soaked T-shirt. A quick inspection allowed her to start breathing again.

She sounded calmer than she was. "It's a flesh wound."

"It burns." Zach tried to look but could not rise off the ground without using the muscles in his midsection that had been torn open.

Laina whipped off her sweater and placed it over both the entry and exit wounds on his right side. Using two hands, one over each hole, she applied pressure. Zach bit back a cry. His breath came in short gasps.

"You're lucky."

"I'd hate to experience what unlucky feels like." He tried to even out his breathing. When he had it under control, he studied her.

Relief washed over her. "The bullet grazed your ribs." If they could get the bleeding stopped quickly, he would be okay. She couldn't say the same for Dan. She had to get over there fast. From the urgent voices in the front yard, it didn't sound good.

"Are you alright?" Zach asked.

She imagined how she must look to him in that moment. Her face surely held no color and her arms, although applying some painful pressure, were shaky.

She met his anxious gaze. "Don't worry about me. I'm made of stern stuff. I need to get over there." She nodded toward Dan Fisher.

"Then go."

"Someone needs to keep the pressure up to stop this bleeding."

Laina silently pleaded with God for help. Sirens wailing were her answer and she closed her eyes momentarily in relief.

In minutes, police were swarming the area. When an officer rushed over to them, she began issuing orders. He took over with Zach and Laina ran to assist with first aid for Dan. She was assured ambulances were close behind and did her best to make sure the sheriff stayed alive to ride in one.

* * *

Logan checked the room number above the door and entered on silent feet. Zach was tucked in bed and sleeping comfortably, despite the usual hospital sounds around him. The single-bed room looked crowded with Caroline asleep in a cushioned chair by the window, her head resting on a pillow jammed against the chair and the windowsill. Laina occupied a plastic chair on the other side of Zach's bed. Her weary gaze was locked on her brother.

Regret washed over him. He never should have brought them along to that house. If he'd just left the job to Nick, none of them would be here right now. But then, Nick might be in the bed before him. His friend had thanked him for watching his back today. Logan didn't know how much of that he'd done. He only knew he hated the troubled crease on Laina's brow.

She sensed movement and glanced his way. Their eyes met and relief flooded her expression. Laina moved quietly from her chair and wrapped her arms around Logan's midsection in a big hug. His heart melted and he hugged her in return. They stood there in silence for several minutes, simply taking comfort in one another. Finally Laina stepped back and looked up into his face.

"I'm so glad you're okay. I couldn't take it if something happened to both of you," she confessed in a soft voice.

Guilt nudged Logan's awareness and his answer was a whisper. "If it wasn't for me, Zach wouldn't be there in the first place."

Zach's skin looked an unhealthy sallow.

"Maybe, but then Nick would be," Laina echoed his earlier thoughts.

Logan ran a distressed hand through his hair. He felt awful.

"Zach's a big boy. If he doesn't want to do something, there's nothing you can do to make him. He went along today because he wanted to. And just think what would have happened if I hadn't come too. Dan might have bled out and died."

"How is he?" Logan crossed to the vacant chair. He sank onto it and stretched out his hand in invitation.

Laina smiled and took it. He drew her onto his lap and she snuggled against him. Arms wrapped around each other, they continued the conversation.

"He's out of surgery and stable. The surgeon was happy with the operation to repair the damage to his chest cavity. The bullet narrowly missed his heart and lodged next to a lung. It's a miracle it didn't hit something vital. He's expected to make a full recovery." One corner of Laina's mouth lifted. "He apparently woke up, flirted with a nurse, and began making retirement jokes."

Logan laughed softly and rested his head against the top of hers. He inhaled deeply. Her hair smelled wonderful and the softness of her body resting against him was a tonic for a terrible day. He'd like it if every day ended this way, with her in his arms.

Laina nestled closely against the solid wall of muscle beneath her cheek and seemed to revel in the warmth of his comforting embrace. "How did things go at the sheriff's office? They kept you there a long time."

"The shooter was killed after a high speed chase." Logan's heart felt black at the knowledge the man hadn't been ready for death when it came for him.

"That's awful!"

He supposed they should hate him after what he'd done. But in light of a lost eternity and Christ's love unfulfilled in the man's life, it just wasn't possible.

"Deputy Smith was grilling the other guy for information when I left."

Laina raised her head off his chest to meet his gaze. "And the house? Did the crime tech guys find what they were after?"

Logan's gaze softened and he gently stroked her cheek. "No. It looks like it's a dead end."

Laina held his gaze, looking delighted by the tender side he now freely expressed.

"Hey," he spoke softly, "do you think you could marry me sometime soon?"

Laina studied his intent green eyes and must have seen no sign of the usual teasing. He supposed she might be cautious or even a bit scared at such a quick proposal. They had only been officially dating for a few days. Yet they'd known each other since they were teenagers and been best friends since high school. They had already discussed almost every conceivable topic during their friendship.

"Are you sure you won't feel cheated later out of our courtship? We haven't really given it any time."

Logan's emerald eyes held hers steadily. "This might sound weird, but I've been courting you a bit at a time since we were kids, getting to know the things you like and dislike. The dreams you have for your future. Wanting a career and someday kids. I've been storing it all up. So although I'm sure there's more to you than I know now, I'd say I've got a better head start for marriage than most."

Laina looked stunned. He knew she had been aware

that he had liked her, but to what extent had been a mystery. Never one to play emotional games, she spoke what was on her mind.

"I will admit that after your conversion you changed. You let me see the real you. By college I was enamored. I was yours if you'd have asked."

He smiled and cupped her cheek with a gentle, work roughened hand. "I'm asking now."

Laina smiled and looked utterly peaceful as she responded. "I will marry you Logan Mathews, you just see if I don't."

His eyes dropped to her lips and she read his intent.

"Maybe hold off on that thought. Your kisses are too nice not to be explored."

Logan's smile was downright flirtatious. "Yours too, Ace."

Laina's brow suddenly puckered curiously. "Why here? Why now?" She gestured to the hospital room occupied by sleeping family members.

Logan let his head fall back with a groan. "I know. Mom would have a fit. I probably should have done it up right, but truth be told, that's not me. I'm ordinary and there's nothing flashy about me. I just wanted it to come from the heart when I was ready." He shrugged apologetically. "I can kneel if you want me to and I'll try again."

Laina chuckled. "No, don't bother. I'm not flashy either. And to be honest, I'm scared stiff of a wedding surrounded by a whole lot of people."

Logan straightened and his eyes lit with common understanding. "Hey, me too."

Laina smiled cheekily. "Wanna elope?"

Logan's lips parted in a mischievous grin. "Okay. But maybe not till Zach can stand on his own two feet. We can have our closest family members. Two, three each tops."

Laina was suddenly enthused with the idea. "And we can invite our friends and extended family to a get together afterward and announce it then."

Logan gave her a squeeze. "I like it."

She leaned back against him, smiling and contented. "Me too."

10

"So what are we looking for anyway?" Logan asked his friend late the next day.

Nick glanced sideways at him and then went back to rifling through kitchen cabinets and draws. "I don't know. Something unusual I guess."

Logan continued picking through a small writing desk by a bay window that looked out over the garden in the backyard. Nothing in the top drawer. He opened the second.

"Where's Laina?" Nick checked the pantry.

The crime scene technicians had conducted a thorough search of the premises and had come up empty handed. Dan had thought him crazy for wanting to search it again himself.

"She's back at work."

Nick's alarmed eyes snapped up and he stared at Logan incredulously. Logan straightened. The desk had yielded nothing.

"Don't worry." He calmly met his friend's gaze. "She's confined to light duties and Nate promised that either he or Gary would be with her at all times."

Nick appeared mollified. "That's good." He finished in the kitchen and moved to the dining room. "Is she driving herself home?"

"Gary promised he'd take her." Logan moved to the dining room also and stood in the center, letting his eyes sweep the room for any kind of anomaly.

"I'm glad she's playing it safe. The way her house looked, and the fact Moretto had the code and waited for Laina to get home..." He shook his head grimly. "He was going to kill her anyway, even before she made him mad."

Logan's gaze swung to Nick and the two locked eyes. "That's what I thought. I didn't tell her that though. I didn't wanna freak her out."

"Me too." Nick opened the bottom cupboard of the display cabinet.

Logan studied its contents through the glass in the top half. "Did the guy we caught yesterday talk?"

"Yeah, but a lot of good it did us. He didn't know Vince from sight. He was contacted by phone and a cash payment was made at a designated drop."

"We know it was Vince. He had the code from Jamison. He didn't wanna get his hands dirty, so he paid a couple of trigger happy punks to do it."

"I'm with you." Nick completed his search there and stood with his hands on his hips. "We just can't prove it."

Logan frowned as he studied the items behind the glass. Fine bone china -probably antique-, crystal glasses, a few ornaments, and a small wooden box. The box was open and resting neatly on blue satin lining was a key.

"That's odd."

Nick followed his line of sight and couldn't seem find anything unusual that would catch Logan's interest. "What?"

Logan pointed. "That."

"It's a key," Nick stated flatly, missing the significance.

Logan sighed with longsuffering. "It's not of any value like everything else in there."

Suspicion crept into Nick's features. "You're right."

The key seemed brand new and there was nothing special about its appearance. Yet there it was on display as though it were an heirloom. He could understand why the crime tech guys had passed over it without a minutes thought. Nick reached in and retrieved the box.

"We may be making something out of nothing."

Logan shrugged. "What have we got to lose?"

Nick lifted the key and passed it to him. He noted it had no markings other than a number. Nick pulled the satin away. He blew out a surprised breath. Beneath it was a logo on a tiny scrap of paper torn presumably from a letterhead. That was unexpected. Logan leaned over to study the image.

"I've seen that logo before."

"Me too. The Walkerville Community Bank."

* * *

Zach sank gratefully into one of his mother's soft recliners and pulled the lever to raise the foot rest. He sighed in contentment. Caroline dropped a blanket over him.

"Can I get you anything?" She had shifted into nursing mode.

Zach's determined gaze met hers. "My laptop. I want to try tracking that IP address again."

Caroline opened her mouth to protest, her usually smiling face scowling in displeasure. "Zach, you were just released from hospital after a gunshot wound! You need to rest."

He looked at her steadily. "Mom, I'll rest when Laina's attacker is caught."

Caroline waved a finger at him. "Now you just leave the detective work to the police and do what your doctor says! You lost a lot of blood yesterday and you went through surgery. They only let you home this soon because there were no complications and I'm a nurse and I said I'd be with you around the clock. What *else* can I get you?"

Zach's eyes took on a steely glint. "Just my laptop."

"Zach-" Caroline was clearly becoming frustrated.

"Mom, someone tried to kill us and my gut tells me Vince Moretto won't stop sending men till he gets what he wants. Now, will you fetch me my laptop or do I have to get it myself?"

They stared at one another in a standoff. Caroline finally conceded and sighed. Zach had always been the most stubborn in the family.

"Fine, but just so you know, I'm not happy about it," she tossed over her shoulder and strode from the room.

"Duly noted." Zach smiled in amusement and waited patiently for her return.

* * *

Nick inserted the key and turned it in the lock. Logan waited with baited breath as his friend opened the safe deposit box. The clerk who had directed them to the correct slot in the wall had left them alone in the vault.

The box slid out and Nick lifted the lid. Logan quirked a curious brow. It was empty, save for one small USB stick. For a moment he doubted this was what had been the cause of yesterday morning's violence.

Nick removed the USB. "You know what strikes me as strange?"

Logan took the box and replaced it in its slot. "What's that?"

"Jamison's great aunt didn't have a computer in her house." A knowing glint sparkled in Nick's eyes.

Logan grinned. "You're right. Let's go visit Zach. I called his mom ten minutes ago and she said he was on his computer tracking down that e-mail."

"I'll check in quickly at the office on our way."

* * *

For a day of light duties, Laina had certainly been busy. There had been several callouts, all relatively easy to deal with. A suspected heart attack, which had turned out to be bad indigestion; a broken wrist from a fall from play equipment in a school yard; and a patient transfer from Walkerville County Hospital to a nursing home in Icy Creek. She had spent the quiet afternoon restocking the ambulance vehicles on standby at their headquarters. She was just filing away her completed inventories in the main office when Gary strode in.

"Time to clock off, Laina. Are you ready to go?"

"Yeah, I'll get my bag now and meet you at your car."

Gary waited by the main desk. "No chance. Your boy-friend made us promise to keep our eyes on you at all times."

Laina had been walking toward the locker room. She paused and glanced back in surprise. "You talked to Logan?"

Gary regarded her carefully. "He called Nate this morning and the boss briefed me on what happened at your place. Why didn't you tell me?"

Laina shrugged. "I didn't want to alarm anyone. I'm sure the worst of it has passed. I'll be back in a minute."

She went to collect her handbag, unsure what to make of her circumstances. It was nice that people cared. However, after her initial panic had subsided, she had concluded that yesterday's incident had been purely a case of being in the wrong place at the wrong time.

She was of no consequence to Vince Moretto now that he had what he wanted. He would be crazy to come after her again merely for revenge. Everything she knew about the case was public knowledge, and his DNA in her house meant that if he was caught, he would be arrested and convicted of assault and attempted murder. He was no fool. There was no reason for him to return.

Laina gathered her things and joined Gary. She would indulge them all for a few days, and then she would put her foot down.

11

One short flight, a ride in a taxi through what had to be the middle of nowhere, and Brylie Montgomery was booking into a rustic bed and breakfast in Icy Creek, Wyoming. However, she didn't try to get comfortable. Her cab was still outside, motor running. After leaving her rather hefty luggage in her small outmoded room, she slid into the back seat of the taxi and gave the driver her next destination.

As he maneuvered the vehicle through the one-horse, country town, she silently fumed. Her mood seesawed swiftly to anxiety. Had Zach received adequate medical care? This place didn't appear to have basic amenities such as decent clothing stores, let alone a proper medical facility. The hospital his mother had mentioned was probably run by hillbillies with slow drawls and cowboy hats, whose only definition of doctoring was leeching.

The cab pulled up in front of a humble white cottage with blue shutters. A small well-kept yard and rose garden was surrounded by a white picket fence. Brylie supposed it could be called charming. Zach had told her of his upbringing, but never in her wildest dreams had she imagined his start in life had been this provincial.

She paid the cab driver and gathered her purse. She gave the pavement a quick sweeping inspection to ensure no animal had left its calling card, and made her way on dangerously high heels to the front door.

* * *

Vince watched from a safe distance as the house went up in smoke. If the cops hadn't found anything on his boss by now, it meant that Jamison had hidden it too well even for them. A mirthless smile lifted one corner of his mouth. Now they would never find it. It was a shame to lose it all, but if it meant covering his tracks, it would be worth it.

He started the engine of the small Honda he had stolen and steered it toward the freeway. There was only one loose end to tie off, and that would be complete by the end of today. One small gift would take care of it, and then it would be time he disappeared for a while.

* * *

Laina breezed in the front door of her mother's home. She heard voices and feminine laughter coming from the kitchen, but spotted Zach working on his laptop in a recliner in the den. She detoured to her left and perched on the arm of his chair.

Zach's intense concentration broke and he glanced

up in surprise. Laina studied the screen he'd been glued to. Making no sense of it, she turned her inspection to his weary face.

"How's the patient?" Her intuitive blue eyes missed nothing.

Zach didn't bother to mask how he was feeling. Instead he shifted the topic. "How was your day?"

"A whole lot better than yours I can see. Why aren't you resting?"

Zach suppressed a smile. "Not you too."

Laina assumed he'd had his quota of smothering, yet was determined to add her portion. "You've got a couple of days worth of stubble, blood shot eyes and pasty skin. Zach, you look like you've been run over by a truck. Why don't you take a nap for a few hours?"

Zach apparently did not miss the fact she hadn't suggested he give up the chase. Every family member understood he had a stubborn streak that would rival a mule.

"In a minute. I just want to finish downloading the documents on this USB. Logan and Nick dropped it off."

Laina's heart skipped a delighted beat. "Logan was here?"

"Ten minutes ago." Zach rubbed tired eyes and watched the download bar edge the last few percentages to the end. "He said he'd stop by later to see you. He mentioned he wanted to clean up first."

Laina's ecstatic expression said it all. She was madly in love and still high on cloud nine.

Zach smiled. He closed the screen. "It does my heart

good to see you so happy."

Laina's brows shot up. "What's with the uncharacter- istic sentimentality?"

Zach closed his eyes and rested his head back. "I'm overtired."

Laina laughed, kissed his cheek and stood. She re- moved the computer from his lap and placed it on the fluffy yellow footstool. When she straightened, her heart gave a jolt when she met a jealous pair of eyes across the living room.

A tall brunette with curls most women would die for, brown eyes framed by long dark lashes and clas- sically beautiful features, stood in the entrance. She wore classy pinstripe pants and a lacy peach top that complimented her trim figure. The elegant woman held two cups of coffee, which were obviously momentarily forgotten. Laina was startled not only by her presence, but by the glacial stare.

How long had she been standing there? Long enough to make the wrong assumption. Amusement replaced Laina's initial alarm.

"Hi, I'm Laina." She hoped to diffuse the awkward moment with a friendly response.

The woman looked instantly relieved. "Oh, Zach's sister, right?"

Laina's eyes twinkled impishly. So this was the infa- mous Brylie Montgomery they had all been hearing about. "Yes. You must be Zach's girlfriend. Mom men- tioned she'd called you last night."

"Yes, she did." The woman placed one of the steaming mugs on the small table beside Zach's chair and took Laina's place on the recliner arm to sip the other.

Laina did not miss the significance of the gesture. The statement of ownership made her somewhat curious. Why was she threatened by a sister? Had Zach told her they were not related by blood?

Laina glanced at Zach only to find a frown of displeasure on his face aimed at his girlfriend. So he had picked up the vibe too. He met Laina's gaze apologetically and she winked. He rolled his eyes with longsuffering and rested his head on the chair back.

"I'll leave you two to catch up." Laina sailed through to the kitchen with a mischievous grin.

* * *

Jamison Harlan was gone. The room the receptionist said he was in had only a vacant bed, neatly made up. What in the world...

So much for his simple plan of entering, injecting an overdose of painkillers into the IV that would inevitably be in the patient's arm, and then slipping out, mission accomplished. Vince ran a frustrated hand through his hair. Had he gotten the room number wrong?

"Put your hands where I can see them," a voice with deadly calm spoke from behind him.

Vince's adrenaline skyrocketed. They had played him.

"How did you know?" he returned with equal composure, buying himself several seconds to think of a way out of this.

The gun in his waistband or the knife in his boot? The gun was his ticket out of here, and he had only a split second before the man behind him would search him and take it.

"Let's just say it was a hunch that paid off," the deputy replied coolly. "Now place your hands behind your head and spread your legs apart."

If he was going to make a move, now was the time. Vince was a hairs breadth away from reaching for his gun when a second and third set of footsteps entered the room. He hesitated.

"Alright, search him Frank."

Vince's features paled. The cop had backup. He gritted his teeth and silently seethed. He would bide his time. His boss would not leave him to rot in prison.

"There's no place you can hold me," Vince stated in a deliberately dispassionate tone. "I'm too valuable to keep on the inside."

Even as one officer's hands searched him and removed his weapons, a threatening presence leaned close and spoke quietly in his left ear.

"Nobody's indispensible. Before long we'll have who you work for too and you'll both be spending a very long time behind bars."

Vince did not like the certainty in the deputy's voice, or the underlying anger. Both promised that this man would hunt down justice to the ends of the earth.

Vince affected a smirk. It would be a merry chase then, because there was no chance this side of eternity that he would ever give up trying to escape. And escaping was something he was good at.

12

"Where've you been?" came the terse question when Logan entered the kitchen via the back door that evening.

Logan sighed and placed his keys on the counter. "Nice to see you too, Dad. Yeah I had a good day. How about you?"

Walter rose from his seat in the den and came to the kitchen. He ignored the sarcasm and went straight to the issue. "You've been gone two nights in a row."

Logan was in no mood to be interrogated. "Is there a question coming anytime soon? Because I'm going out again as soon as I've showered."

Walter's eyes narrowed dangerously. "Don't sass me, boy. I'm still your father."

Logan moved around the counter and stood face to face with his dad. He may have aged and even claimed to have accepted Christ, but he was still a bully and Logan would have none of it.

"Yes, you're my father. But I'm also a grown man and you're under my roof. I'll do what I please when I please and thank you not to grill me about it."

Walter's eyes flickered with something Logan did not like. However, Walter had the good sense to back off. He sat on a stool at the counter and toyed with an empty beer bottle, idly spinning it around.

"I saw you with her, you know."

Logan's internal radar immediately sent out a warning. "With who?"

"That girl you used to like in high school. What was her name again?" Walter searched his memory. He smiled when he had it. "Laina."

The unpleasant gleam of power in his father's eyes made Logan's blood boil. It was like a cat toying with a mouse.

"Have you been following me?" Logan's tone was ominously low.

Walter caught it and brushed off Logan's concern with a wave of his hand. "Stop being so prickly. I was at the hardware store seeing about a job and saw the two of you up the street near Gracie's the other day."

Logan rummaged for an apple in the bottom of the refrigerator.

"What of it?"

He came up empty. Walter had eaten everything there was and failed to replenish it. Logan closed the fridge door and leaned against its smooth cool surface. He crossed his arms over his chest in a casual stance.

"You say you're a Christian, so you should know what the Bible says about sleeping with a woman you're not married to." Walter's dirty assumption was issued with a frank stare.

Logan couldn't believe his ears. Of all the people to start judging him! He silently regarded his father.

Something in Logan's spirit did not sit right where Walter was concerned.

"Let's cut to the chase, Dad." Logan held his gaze and decided to tackle the situation head on. "You think pointing out morality and Scripture will convince me you're a Christian, but it won't. I'm not fooled by your pious act. Mom may be, but this is the way I figure it...

"You got down on your luck or ran into some sort of money trouble. You hightailed it back here with this concocted story, hoping she'd believe you've changed and take you in. Well it won't wash with me for two simple reasons: I still see no love in you for anyone here but yourself, and there are times your eyes betray you."

Walter's face became mottled red and he rose swiftly from the stool and stalked around the counter toward his son. Logan took a challenging step forward and waited, arms by his side.

"Just like now," he stated calmly.

Walter moved to within an inch of him, eyes spitting fire. "What kind of a Christian speaks to his father that way?"

"The kind that won't be walked upon," Logan replied with steely resolve. "You've got a week to get a job and move out. And remember, if you lay one hand on Mom or Tia, I'll have you up on assault charges."

Walter's pupils constricted and his skin grew even redder. Rage was a good word to describe what Logan was staring down. He shook his head sadly and turned away, striding to the bedroom hallway just off the kitchen.

He turned in the doorway and found his father right where he'd left him. Walter's eyes bored into his, but he wisely kept his mouth shut. The man obviously knew he had a tenuous line to tread.

"And for what it's worth, I was with Laina, but not in the way you think. We spent the first night watching old movies with her family, and the second we spent in hospital by her brother's bedside." With that simple explanation, Logan left to go clean up.

The sooner he was out of this place the better.

* * *

"Okay God," Zach whispered into the dark room, "what now?"

No answer immediately sprang to mind. It was well past midnight and the house was silent around him. He was in his old room, as comfortable as pillows and rugs could make him. However, the painkillers were wearing off. He stared at the ceiling touched by shadows from moonlight seeping between the curtains. Zach found it a little eerie.

He had been putting on a brave face for everyone, but when the darkness and silence pressed in on him like this, it was hard not to see flash backs. He had prayed his way through them. Now the fear had abated and he was left with the other events of the day to deal with. He found evaluating his life a whole lot trickier than chasing down an online predator.

His door inched open with a creak. Zach's head swiveled in that direction, his heart pumping furiously. He breathed a sigh of relief when Laina slipped into his room.

He flicked the bedside lamp on and smiled at the cute picture she made. She was wearing a pair of his mother's crazy cartoon pajamas and carrying a glass of water. Her long blond hair was sleep tussled and in a riot around her shoulders.

Laina sat on the edge of his bed and wordlessly handed him some painkillers and the water glass. Raising himself up off the pillow enough to drink was painful and awkward, and left him out of breath by the time he laid back down. He handed her the glass, which she placed on the nightstand. They regarded one another in silence for several minutes.

"You look awful," she finally spoke. "How are you doing?"

Zach sighed. There was no escaping her intuitive evaluation. She'd always been able to see right through him.

"Sore, a bit scared, and totally lost."

Laina simply nodded and waited for him to go on.

"What am I supposed to do?"

Laina seemed to puzzle until she caught on that he was not referring to his injury, or to the case. "Brylie?"

Zach sighed again and nodded, feeling one hundred years old. "Things back home were going great up until I told her I was coming here and invited her for the weekend. She was like the ice queen. Now that I'm re-covering from a gunshot wound, she's all clingy. I can't figure her out. I can't figure us out."

"Maybe you're not supposed to."

Zach pondered that remark and the implications it had for his life.

"She's flashy, that's for sure. And she's certainly threatened by me."

The rest of the evening had gone relatively smooth, except for the subtle efforts the other woman had made during conversations to make evident her claim on Zach.

"That's another thing I don't get. You and I are not related by blood, but we're as close to being brother and sister as anyone can be. Yet somehow the fact you're beautiful and we're close bothers her."

Laina was warmed by Zach's observation. "You think I'm beautiful?"

Zach's eyes gleamed mischievously. "Sure, but I don't let that fool me anymore."

Laina smothered a smile. "Typical."

Zach's mind returned to his girlfriend and the humor in his eyes evaporated.

"I thought she was the one, but lately all she's done is push me to excel in a career I'm finding less and less appealing."

"Money and status seem to be a big deal to her."

When Zach looked at her in surprise, she went on to explain.

"I saw it in her clothes and her shoes. They're top

brand name items, and the way she subtly disdains all things country reminds me of you when you first got here."

Zach's smile was broad. "I guess I was a bit of a city brat."

Laina chuckled. "A bit? I would have used the word 'total'."

A comfortable silence settled as they remembered the beginning of their friendship. It had been adventurous, that was for sure.

"If God wanted you to marry this woman, Zach, it would have been confirmed to you in lots of different ways."

That caught Zach's interest. "In what ways?"

"Oh let me think..." Laina's thoughtful gaze drifted. "Scriptures would stand out to you, and not just in your personal reading. The same ones would come through sermons at church, friends and family. Every action we take must line up with God's guidelines stated in the Bible. Then there's the way God speaks through how we feel. You would feel a sense of complete peace. You would just know that you know that you know. There's many more ways. Those are just the ones that I can think of at the moment."

Zach pondered Laina's advice and had to admit to himself that he hadn't had any of those happen to him concerning Brylie.

"She has to know Jesus too, Zach, or she'll be constantly pulling you in a different direction to the one you know God is calling you."

Zach met his sister's honest gaze and knew she'd hit the nail on the head. Brylie confessed to be a Christian, but her priorities and dreams for their future were far different from his. It became painfully clear to him why he had been so unsettled for the past week. It had been staring him in the face all along, only he had been too busy to pay attention. God had been talking and he had failed to listen.

"Thanks, Laina. I've got some thinking I want to do." He squeezed her hand on the cover between them and she smiled in understanding.

"I'll be praying for you," she assured him and quietly left.

Zach's heart turned to God once again, only this time his prayer was different. "Okay God, how do I go about this?"

He took his worn copy of the Bible he'd read since he was a teen from the top drawer of his bedside table. Not sure exactly where to start, he simply read whatever page fell open.

* * *

Laina could not shake the burden on her heart for her brother. Beside Logan, Zach was her dearest friend. He was in turmoil and her heart wrung with compassion for him. She directed her thoughts to her heavenly Father.

Lord God, my heart is hurting so much for Zach. He's

in a rut that only You can see a way clear of. Please show him his next step and give him the courage to take it?

Unable to sleep now, Laina picked up one of Caroline's old Bibles. She flicked to a passage she had been reading recently and simply opened herself to listen for whatever God had on His mind. Several chapters in Isaiah later, her eyes were growing heavy. Suddenly a verse seemed to come alive and leap off the page like an arrow to her heart. Drowsiness evaporated.

'1 The Spirit of the Lord God is upon me; because the Lord hath anointed me to preach good tidings unto the meek; he hath sent me to bind up the brokenhearted, to proclaim liberty to the captives, and the opening of the prison to them that are bound;

2 To proclaim the acceptable year of the Lord, and the day of vengeance of our God; to comfort all that mourn;

3 To appoint unto them that mourn in Zion, to give unto them beauty for ashes, the oil of joy for mourning, the garment of praise for the spirit of heaviness; that they might he called trees of righteousness, the planting of the Lord, that he might be glorified.'

The last part of verse three spoke to Laina the most. She had read this portion of Scripture a lot over the years, and understood that it was a prophecy about the coming Savior Jesus Christ. However, on a personal note, she could now see how it also applied to her and to all Christians alike. She even recalled seeing the word 'trees' substituted in one of the different Bibles she had at home for 'oak'.

Enthused by the discovery and deeply curious about what she sensed God saying to her, Laina got up from the mattress on the study floor and sat at the computer desk. She took a pen from the tin next to the screen and snatched a sheet of A4 from the printer to jot down her reflections.

'The oak is usually a solitary tree. Its roots go down deep and expand to the portion and dimensions of that which we see above ground, if not bigger. It is strong, solid, unmovable. It bends and flexes in the wind, but not so much that it breaks or sheds limbs.

It undergoes changes with the seasons. Barren it stands in winter, wind whistling through its bare branches. In spring it comes to life with shoots of green. In summer it provides shade and respite from unrelenting sunshine. It is a source of food for foraging creatures with its multitude of acorns. Other animals enjoy its green leaves for nourishment.

The oak stands as a windbreak to protect everything around it, shielding people, animals and structures from the brunt of otherwise devastating winds. It is fire retardant and can withstand intense heat. Steady and unchanging it stands, through all seasons, and over generations. It does not shrink or wither away. It merely continues its constant cycle of steady growth until what began as an acorn becomes a mammoth tree.

All of these are interesting characteristics to bear in mind when we read Isaiah 61:3, where God's people are referred to as "... trees of righteousness, the planting of the Lord, that He might be glorified." The word "trees" here means strength; hence, anything strong, such as an oak or other strong tree.

We Christians are to have a deep root system that draws spiritual nourishment from Jesus Christ and His living word on a daily basis. We must be strong and unmovable when faced with hardship and temptation. At times in life we will feel barren and empty, even lonely or sad. However, we must never feel lost, for we are planted where we are by God for a time and a purpose. We may not always know what that is, but then you never see an oak looking uncertain of its position or its existence. It just is, and it dominates its surroundings.

Like the oak, we are to provide spiritual and emotional respite and nourishment for those who come to us for shelter. As we draw our own nourishment from Christ Himself, the Holy Spirit will bring 'fruits' naturally into being for others to partake of. Our version of 'acorns and leaves' may be encouragement, peace, joy, love, faithfulness, meekness, patience, kindness, goodness, gentleness, longsuffering and self control. What others draw from us helps them to refresh, recover, be challenged and to grow.

Like the oak, we Christians firmly planted where the Lord wants us, will not bend and break under the pressure of life. We are flexible, and instead provide a buffer from the devastating 'winds' of life for those around us. We are not afraid of storms, or uprooted by them. We remain firm and steadfast, anchored down deep in Christ. When fiery trials come, we are not scorched. Simultaneously, we shield those close to us from the flames. We are to be a place of comfort and rest. And when all is said and done, we accomplish that purpose for which God planted us where we are, in our time.

We are His oaks of righteousness, the planting of the Lord, that He might be glorified in and through us.'

Encouraged and challenged by the new perspective, Laina wanted to share her thoughts with her brother. She folded the paper and tiptoed to Zach's room. She slipped inside. His light was on, but he was fast asleep, his Bible resting open on his chest.

Laina smiled, pleased he was finally getting some rest. She gently removed it from his fingers and sat it on his nightstand. She placed her reflections on top and switched the light off.

Help him rest well, Lord? she silently requested and left as quietly as she'd come.

13

"How are you feeling today, Laina?" her boss asked on his way into his office.

Nate leaned against the doorframe casually. In full uniform, he was just as ruggedly handsome as the day he had saved her life ten years ago. He was also the same loveable rogue he had always been.

Laina had commandeered his computer to quickly check her mail between callouts. She glanced up from the screen and smiled.

"I'm fine. How's Jen?" she inquired about his wife of nine years.

Nate's easy going smile broadened and his eyes lit with a warm glow. "She's as gorgeous as the day I married her."

Laina smiled in return, pleased he had someone who made him so happy. "And the kids?"

"Ellie is six and a chatterbox, and Corey is five months old. He had his first taste of real food yesterday. The little guy couldn't get enough of it."

Laina remembered seeing them last month and had been surprised at their fast growth. She clicked open her inbox on the computer and started with the top message. It was from Nate.

"Did I miss something in the supply order?" Laina asked him as she began reading.

Nate frowned. "No, why?"

Laina's blood ran cold. Nate must have watched as all color drained from her face, because he came away from the doorframe and into the room.

"What's wrong?" He studied her horrified expression and alarm entered his eyes.

Laina pushed away from the computer desk. She stood and moved back so that he could see the missive on the screen.

"The sender is supposed to be you," she explained with dismay. "Take a look."

Nate's puzzled frown evaporated when he read the e-mail in her inbox. His eyes lit with anger and heat crept into his tanned cheeks.

'You lied and now you'll pay. You won't know where. You won't know when. And he won't be there to save you.'

"Who could have sent this?" His cool tone belied the protective surge evident in his steely countenance. "The guy that attacked you?"

Laina was stunned by the change. She had never seen Nate angry, let alone looking furious enough to throttle someone.

"I don't know, but it was done just like the first."

Nate turned to stare at her incredulously. "You mean you've had more than one threat by e-mail?"

Her past reared its ugly head and Laina wanted to back away from him. His anger was almost palpable.

That it was not directed at her made little difference. He was male and he was livid.

Nate must have seen a flicker of fear in her eyes and worked to tamp down his fury. "I'm not mad at you, Laina."

She drew a steadying breath and tried to override her age-old reaction. "I know."

Nate waited patiently for a reply. When none was forthcoming, he asked again. "Could this be from your attacker?"

Laina swallowed hard and fought to remain calm. "We thought so, now I'm not so sure. What does he mean by me lying? The only times I spoke with Vince Moretto were on the phone about a coded note, and when he broke into my house."

Nate's lips were set in a grim line as he reached for the office phone. He punched in some numbers. Laina wondered who he might be calling. She got her answer seconds later when someone on the other end picked up and she heard Nate greet Nick Foster and explain the situation.

"Yeah, she's thinking it was Vince Moretto, but isn't sure about the reference to lying. ... When?" Nate's disturbed gaze held Laina's.

Her stomach churned ominously and she wanted to be sick. She settled for circling the desk and sitting in one of the two chairs facing her boss who was still standing. She wrapped her arms around her squeamish midsection and waited for the conversation to finish.

"Yeah, I'd appreciate that. I'll forward it now. ... Why

to Zach Delaney? ... Well that's something. Let's hope this one turns up a lead. ... Okay, thanks Deputy." Nate hung up.

He stared silently at Laina for several seconds before dropping into the computer chair. He forwarded the message as promised and finally sat back and studied her.

"What was all of that about Zach?"

"Nick said Zach finally traced the exact computer the last e-mail was sent from. It was the library in Icy Creek."

Hope lifted Laina's spirit. Nate looked as though he felt bad about delivering the news, but she needed to hear it.

"Nick said he checked the log book at the library for the time and date the e-mail was sent, even the security camera by the door. Nothing. Whoever sent it knew how to cover his tracks."

Laina ventured an optimistic comment. "Maybe he might have slipped up this time and Zach will find him?"

"Maybe, but it won't be Vince Moretto he finds. He was arrested during an attempt to silence Jamison Harlan, the undercover cop you helped pull from the wreckage."

Laina digested this in silence. If it wasn't Vince sending the threats, then still out there somewhere was a stalker. And she had no idea how she could have attracted his ire.

It had been simple really. Vince masked a smug smile behind the latex face as he climbed awkwardly into his partner's old model Ford sedan. He sighed wearily with the effort, still completely in character.

His comrade helped buckle Vince's belt and closed his door, playing the part of caring son to the hilt. Once behind the wheel, Pietro Moretto calmly started the engine and put the car in gear. He steered his way clear of the downtown county police office and navigated busy city streets.

A car change and another identity alteration later and they were both headed to their safe house.

* * *

"You're kidding!" Laina was surprised to say the least.

"Identity theft is a major key to accessing funds and gaining control of vital interests," Zach reasoned from his comfortable recliner where Brylie had tucked a rug around him. "It's a big issue because everything nowadays is computerized."

Logan shifted forward on the couch, elbows on his knees. "So let me get this straight," he clarified for the stunned gathering in Caroline's den, "Vince Moretto is trafficking fake I.D's?"

"That's why you got shot?" Brylie looked appalled

someone would go to such a length over a collation of personal information on a USB.

She was perched on the arm of Zach's chair. Caroline occupied the large fluffy yellow footstool, the cup of coffee in her hands forgotten. Logan and Laina were side by side on the couch, and Nick sat in the other recliner looking tired beyond his years. The extra duties were obviously taking their toll.

"Zach was shot because he was in the wrong place at the wrong time," he countered. "We walked in on Vince's gofers while they were looking for the information Jamison had hidden."

"But like everyone else, they didn't know what they were looking for," Logan surmised. "Who would have suspected a small key in a china cabinet?"

Zach closed his laptop and Brylie automatically stepped in and took it from him so that he wouldn't have to move. She carefully placed it on the floor beside his chair, and returned to his side.

Zach rubbed bloodshot eyes and then ran a hand across his face. He ignored her close vigil and continued his explanation.

"It contained lots of profiles on people. I found names, addresses, phone numbers, bank account details, billing account numbers, birth and marriage certificates, passports, even seemingly inconsequential details. Things like the person's preferred dress code, children, pets, and things they did in their spare time. Basically everything someone would need to either impersonate them, rip them off, or enough to sell via the black market for someone else to do it."

Caroline was confused and her face said as much. "But why would someone want to buy identities?"

"Perhaps to exit and enter the country illegally, or to cover their own tarnished identity. With the right information, the wrong person can gain access to financial institutions, buy or sell businesses and properties that don't belong to them. You name it and it can be done," Nick elaborated. "The information on that USB is worth a fortune to whoever Vince Moretto works for, which is why he would stop at nothing to get it back. We suspect he's the one who burned down Jamison's aunt's house."

Logan sat back on the couch and draped an arm around Laina's shoulder. "Good thing he's behind bars then, hey."

Nick shifted uncomfortably in his chair, his expression telling. "That's actually why I stopped by."

Logan's gaze narrowed.

Nick had to force the bad news from his lips. "He escaped from police custody today."

"What?"

"How?"

"That's impossible!"

The room erupted in simultaneous outrage. Logan sprang from his seat, while Zach pulled himself up a little straighter. Laina paled significantly and Caroline cast her a worried glance.

Nick waved for silence in the barrage that followed. "Deputy Brian Smith is heading the case. He called me this afternoon out of courtesy because he thought you all needed to know you should lock your doors and move around with a little more caution than usual."

Logan ran an aggravated hand through his hair and glanced anxiously down at the woman he loved. They were obviously both thinking the same thing. Vince had promised to repay her. Would he make good his threat?

"How could the police make such a debacle of this?"

Laina frowned at him. "Since when do you use the word debacle?"

A glint of amusement made his green eyes sparkle. "What? You think I don't look up those weird words you like to use?"

Zach restrained an abrupt laugh before it could send tendrils of pain shooting through his side. Nick hid a smile and rose.

"At the moment Deputy Smith thinks Vince is a part of a theft ring and has been put with another partner. Possibly the same one that helped him escape the bus crash."

"How did it happen?" Caroline wondered aloud. "I thought Vince was supposed to be in prison?"

"It doesn't work that way, Mrs. Delaney," Nick explained patiently, one thumb looped through his uniform belt.

"Then where was he when he escaped?"

Nick met Brylie's concerned gaze as he answered. "He was in the interrogation room in the Cody County Police Office. The deputies interviewing him were called out momentarily when his lawyer arrived and requested a private moment alone with his client. The officers were obliged to give it to him.

"There was a commotion in the main room that cleared out the officers behind the one way glass in the interview room. Before anyone knew what had happened, the camera in the interrogation room was down and so was the guard outside the door."

Everyone in the room listened to this explanation in a mixture of astonishment and anger.

"It all happened in a matter of minutes. When officers realized Vince was missing and so was his lawyer, they locked down the building and searched everywhere. They found the lawyer's briefcase empty and both men's clothes, all dumped in the interrogation room. An adjacent office window was open that an officer swore had been closed minutes before.

"Deputy Smith examined security camera footage later and noticed an old man and younger man with him unaccounted for walking directly past the frey toward that office. Neither face matched Vince or the lawyer's, but the case and clothes suggest that both men are not only into identity theft, but are masters of disguise."

Zach's brows shot up. Logan cast a troubled look at his intended and sank down beside her. That meant anyone on the street or on a call out could be Vince, and they'd never know it until it was too late.

"Do you think that e-mail could have been from Vince, seeing that he wasn't in police custody like we thought?" Laina asked, hoping that was the case. If not, they would have two nasty pieces of work on the loose and likely after her.

Nick's look was apologetic. "Sorry Laina, but he was still in a cell when that threat was sent. That's the other reason I came."

He held her gaze and the grim set of his mouth and the muscle twitch in his jaw gave her a sense of unease.

"There are two men out there now who hate me, aren't there?" She felt a rock plummet to the bottom of her stomach. *Be an oak, be an oak,* she mentally bolstered her sagging spirit.

"It seems so," Nick confirmed her fear. "Lock your doors and don't go anywhere without someone with you, preferably a guy. You might even consider getting a small handgun."

Laina's insides recoiled. She could never shoot someone. She was in the business of saving lives, not taking them. "I won't carry a weapon."

"Then stay with Logan, and when you're at work, stick by Nate or Gary." He crossed to the door. He paused with his hand on the doorknob. "At least pack some mace in your purse." He quietly left.

Silence reigned in his wake.

Caroline sat her cup aside and slapped her knees. "Anyone up for pizza?"

The two couples looked at her as though she had lost her mind.

Zach appeared astounded. "Didn't you just hear

what Nick said, Mom?"

Caroline stood and met her son's gaze with a serious one of her own. "Yes I did, and I'll be sleeping with a baseball bat under my bed and so will you and Laina. I also think it's time we all eat. A full stomach and some time to pray will put some perspective on the situation." She wandered to the kitchen.

Zach sighed and wearily rubbed his face again. He evidently needed a decent night's sleep and it didn't look like he was going to get one anytime soon. "You're right."

Brylie silently collected empty mugs from around the room and followed Caroline. Zach observed her brooding expression and so did Laina. Their relationship was a ticking time bomb and she sensed that Zach had the heavy burden of being the one responsible to detonate it. He needed a holiday on a beach somewhere far away.

"I'll head out for a bit and see what I can find at the hardware store to tighten security around here," Logan announced and stood. "Will you be okay for half an hour while I'm gone?"

Laina quashed the fear rising within her and offered a reassuring smile. "I'll be fine. There's four of us and at least three of us can wield a bat or throw something heavy."

Logan's displeased frown cut straight through her attempt at levity. "Do not answer the door to anyone you don't recognize, you hear me?"

Laina's brows arched at his sudden commanding

tone. "Yes sir!" She added a cheeky salute, hoping to lighten the mood.

Logan smothered a smile. "I mean it, Ace. If you go outside or answer that door to a stranger I'll-"

Laina stood and faced him with a smug glint in her eyes. "You'll what?"

Zach caught another laugh before it could escape and grinned at the exchange.

Logan pointed a finger. "I'll think of something." He strode to the door and opened it. "Stay put."

Laina poked her tongue out at him. He shook his head as he exited. She turned to her brother.

"You don't look so good. Is it time for your meds?" She felt his forehead. Good, no fever.

"Not for another hour. I'm just tired." Zach studied her and was suddenly struck by gratitude for the day she had walked into his life. "I love you, sis'."

Laina was taken aback. He rarely ever said those words.

"Wow, that close brush with death has softened you up a bit, Zach." She ruffled his hair.

Zach smiled. "I guess it has. Thanks for the oak tree thing."

Laina dropped a kiss on his cheek. "You're welcome. I hoped it might encourage you a bit."

"It did. I was reading Isaiah sixty-one just before I fell asleep. How's that for timing?"

"God's timing, not mine." She started for the kitchen. "I'm headed to lock down the house. See if you can catch some rest before the pizza arrives."

"Fat chance."

She understood. Brylie would no doubt be back by his side in a matter of minutes smothering him, and if she did not miss her guess, there was an unpleasant discussion they were destined to have.

14

Brylie eased away from the doorway to the den and tried to look busy washing mugs at the kitchen sink. Laina had kissed him. On the cheek or not, Brylie was not happy. Those two were in complete denial of their true feelings and it was time to confront the situation head on. She silently fumed while she washed the last cup.

Caroline had gone with Laina to check windows and doors, leaving Brylie a rare moment alone with Zach. She strode purposefully into the den and drew the fluffy footstool in front of Zach's chair.

* * *

Zach watched Brylie's swift movements and knew the time of reckoning had come. She sat facing him and they regarded one another quietly.

"What's going on between you and Laina?"

Zach's brow furrowed. He had not expected a blunt approach. Brylie was usually subtle in addressing her concerns. Laina's words regarding his girlfriend's insecurity replayed in his mind.

"She's my sister."

"We both know that's not true." Her brown eyes had hardened.

Zach was not up to a confrontation. But better to end it now than waste her time and his with a relationship that was clearly going nowhere.

"Your jealousy is leading you to see things that are simply not there. Leave my sister out of this. Our problems have nothing to do with her."

Brylie's eyes sparked fire. "Our problems? Things between us were going just fine until you decided to put your career in jeopardy and have a holiday." Her hands rose in disdain.

Zach sighed. "My career..." He let the thought dangle. Did he want a future in design and programming? With sudden clarity he finally understood the culmination of his discontent.

"You know, I don't want to go back to my job and I don't think I even want to go back to New York. I love it here, and despite all that's happened, I've really enjoyed putting my computer skills to use helping Nick find Laina's stalker. I have purpose here." He dared to bare his soul. "I've been miserable in my job and miserable in New York for a while now, and it wasn't until I came here that I understood why."

Zach looked into two beautiful, angry brown eyes and prayed she would understand that this was not a personal attack.

"So I make you miserable, is that it? And you think Laina and this small blip on a map can make you happy?"

Zach wanted to howl with frustration. He managed to keep his voice calm as he concluded. "We have no common goals or dreams. It's your way or the highway, and in me trying to fit into your vision of our happy life together, I've lost the most important person in my life."

Brylie's eyes narrowed dangerously. "Laina."

Zach appealed to her logic. "No. God. When was the last time we went to church together? Or prayed as a couple for that matter?"

She was having none of it. Brylie Montgomery rose from her seat on the ridiculous looking footstool and stared down at him with contempt.

"Don't you dare make this about God when we both know who the real problem is!"

Zach pushed angrily from his chair and stood on weak legs. His color drained with the pain and his head spun from a drop in blood pressure. However by sheer fortitude, he remained upright.

"Laina has been through more than you'll likely ever experience in your lifetime, so kindly keep your re-marks to me and the issue at hand."

"When are you going to see that she is the issue?" Brylie's look was scathing. "You-" She bit back the dis-tasteful word she clearly wanted to say and spun. She stormed for the door, grabbing her purse from the small table in the entrance against the wall. She turned to glare at him.

"Call me when you come to your senses." She opened the door.

Resignation came over Zach in a tide of emotion. "I'm sorry it has to end this way," he spoke gently. "I just hope you can forgive me."

* * *

The air left Brylie's lungs in a rush. He was breaking up with her. The nerve! She stepped out the open door and slammed it shut in her wake.

She planned to thoroughly shake the dust of this crummy little town off her feet and get on the next plane to civilization. But not before dealing with the woman who had caused her hopes and dreams to crumble.

* * *

Laina heard raised voices and left Caroline gathering in the washing from the line out back. She heard the front door slam shut and entered the living room. Her perplexed gaze landed upon her brother standing in front of the recliner he had claimed. She noted with alarm that he was visibly shaking.

"Zach, what's wrong? What just happened?" She crossed the room as she spoke and placed both hands on his shoulders. She gently eased him back into the chair. That he did not fight her spoke volumes.

"Brylie's gone."

"Why?" Laina sat on the stool the other woman had

vacated and stared into his colorless features with concern.

Zach leaned forward and rested his face in his hands, then cringed and clutched his side. He would not look at her, which worried her even more.

"Did you have a fight?"

Zach nodded and gingerly leaned back in the chair. He finally met her gaze. "I broke it off."

Understanding was swift in coming. She had sensed it coming, but hadn't realized it would happen so swiftly. Compassion welled within her for her brother.

"You were right about her insecurity. She thinks we've got something going."

"Well she was right," Laina affirmed adamantly.

Zach's heart lurched. "What?"

Steel entered Laina's gaze. "We're siblings. You can't get much thicker than that."

Zach's mouth tipped in a half smile. "You know what I meant."

"I know. I'm sorry, Zach. It must be really hard."

Zach's head rested against the soft chair and his expression was thoughtful. "You know, it's strange. I'm starting to feel peaceful. How is that possible?"

Laina smiled gently. "You're starting down a new path God wants you to tread. He's letting you know it's the right one."

Zach's head lifted and he stared at her in surprise. He returned her smile and appeared to be considering her words as she squeezed his knee and stood. An unearthly sense of rightness came over his countenance and she felt the burden she had been carrying regarding his unhappiness begin to lift. He was going to be okay.

* * *

Laina had gone too far. It was time to show her the extent to which her behavior had affected others. Two hands carefully dipped the scalpel in the bottom of the steak tray. It emerged covered in blood. Perfect. This would send a very clear message that she had better let him go.

She had inflicted too much pain. If she backed off from *him*, then forgiveness was possible. But if not, there would be swift justice. Such betrayal demanded it.

* * *

Nick began at the top of Zach's long list. Surely at least one of the people whose lives had been documented on the USB had seen or heard something unusual. He was hoping for something useful such as any unaccounted for bank withdrawals, or a description of someone seen loitering near their home or workplace. Each person had been under intense scrutiny for quite some time. Surely Vince had made a mistake somewhere along the line.

Nick hoped that with some phone calls and a few visits to the folk on the list over the next few days, he might be able to turn up something that would give them a lead in this case. He picked up the office phone and dialed the first number.

* * *

Laina opened the door with a welcoming smile. Logan frowned.

"I thought I told you not to answer the door to anyone, Ace."

Laina shrugged and reached up on tip toe to plant a kiss on his cheek. "I didn't think that included you."

Logan stepped over the threshold carrying a bag from the hardware store in one hand and his tool box in the other. "And what if it hadn't been me?"

"I could see you coming up the path through the living room window," she replied logically and started to close it again.

Logan shook his head and traipsed through to the kitchen where he could smell fresh pizza. Laina was about to close the door when a flash of white caught her eye. Whatever it was, Logan had walked straight over it. She glanced down.

A small note lay on the doorstep. The letters were of various sizes and styles, all cut and pasted from a newspaper. A bloody scalpel lay atop the missive.

Laina didn't know which freaked her out more. The obvious threat to her life, or the chilling words.

'LeT hiM GO Or YOu WiLl pAy.'

Numbness stole over her. He had been here in person and nobody had noticed. She glanced up at the empty street. No unusual cars or people were hanging around. Laina's gaze dropped again to the note and the scalpel. Whose blood was that? She swallowed hard and fought a sudden wave of dizziness.

"Be an oak, be an oak, be an oak," she muttered to herself and drew several quick breaths to rid the spots from dancing before her eyes.

Caroline chuckled behind her. "What on earth are you saying?"

Laina stepped away from the door and grabbed her mobile from the hall table. Caroline watched her shaking hands punch in a phone number and observed her ashen face.

Her puzzled gaze searched the street and then the yard through the open door. Nothing was amiss. Then her eyes dropped and she spotted it. She moved forward and reached down to pick it up.

"Don't touch that!" Laina barked sharply.

Caroline's hand pulled away as though burned. Her wide eyes met her daughter's.

"There may be fingerprints or something the police can use to find whoever left it," she explained more gently with the mobile to her ear.

A male voice picked up on the other end of the line and Laina drew a controlled breath.

Be calm and don't panic.

"Icy Creek Sheriff's Department, Deputy Nick Foster speaking."

Strength rose from somewhere deep inside and Laina responded in a steady voice. "Nick, the stalker's been here."

* * *

"One more time in the slammer and you're finished, Moretto!"

The loud thump of his boss's fist connecting with the solid oak desk punctuated the angry statement. Vince inwardly cringed. He knew the man well enough to know it was no empty threat.

"Because of your bungle, the authorities know about our operation. Your thirst for revenge has compromised everything I've worked to build!"

Vince stared into a pair of dark eyes. They were spitting fire, and only a fool would cross the middle aged man behind them.

"The police know nothing. Their interview questions showed they have no idea what we're pedaling, which means they didn't find the stash in that old house." Vince rose from his seat.

"Where do you think you're going?" The man was astonished. He had obviously barely begun the tongue lashing he intended to give.

Vince reached for the heavy wooden study door and turned with his hand on the brass knob. "I've had eyes on that old house twenty-four/seven. The cops may not have found the stash, but there were two men who came to search the following day. I'll just make doubly sure they came up empty too before I begin building another portfolio."

His boss's icy stare narrowed. "And what makes you think you still have a job?"

Vince met his glacial gaze with a steady one of his own. "I'm too good at what I do to not be valuable to you."

Chilling eyes regarded him and finally one corner of the man's lips lifted ever so slightly. "Nobody is indispensible, Moretto. Just you remember that the next time your lust for blood threatens to override your common sense."

"Got it."

"And this time leave Jamison Harlan to me. Who were the two men?"

Vince's fingers dropped from the handle. "I don't know their names yet, but I'll have details for you by nightfall."

"Good."

Vince quietly left. This was his last chance, and he didn't plan on messing it up.

15

"Okay, let's make a list of people who might have any reason to hold a vendetta," Nick suggested.

It was late and he was now off duty and in jeans and a T-shirt, sitting with Logan, Zach and Laina around the dining room table. Caroline was bustling about the kitchen nearby making coffees for everyone.

"We need to be even more specific than that," Logan asserted. "Whoever this is, they have something against Laina being with me."

"So someone with a possible infatuation," Nick concluded.

"Or someone who thinks Laina and I have a thing for each other," Zach commented quietly.

All eyes swiveled to him in bewilderment. Only Laina's held comprehension. Brylie's heated jealousy was still fresh in her mind.

"Who would be daft enough to think that?" Nick's disbelieving expression said he thought such a person mad.

"Brylie," Laina supplied. "She's incredibly insecure where Zach and I are concerned."

Nick quirked one eyebrow. "Are you serious?"

Caroline sat the coffee jar on the counter and rested

her hands either side of it, facing the group. "I noticed it too."

"But lowering herself to sending threatening e-mails and leaving a note and scalpel like that... She'd have to be pretty twisted." Logan was apparently not inclined to think she could stoop so low.

Laina didn't think so either, but her anger before her departure was unnerving.

"We can't rule anyone out at this stage."

"Zach's right," Nick agreed. "Anybody with anything against Laina needs to be on this list."

"As for motive, Brylie's got plenty. She's bristled at every mention of Laina our entire relationship, and at the moment, she's the woman scorned."

Laina silently contemplated Zach's reluctant admission. That he would put his ex-girlfriend's name forward as a threat spoke volumes.

Nick quickly scrawled her name at the top of his notepad and looked up at the group. "Alright, who's next?"

"The scalpel is a direct threat to your life, and it says the stalker knows you're a paramedic. Any casualties you've handled that haven't done so well, or may have even developed a crush on you? Or families of a patient that hasn't survived?" Logan directed his question to Laina.

She shook her head. "There's been a lot, but no one who would blame me for their misfortune. As for crushes, I deal with people for such a short time and then hand them over to the hospital. There's no time for any real follow up where an infatuation could develop."

"You never know what's in the mind of another person," Nick remarked.

Laina sighed and tucked her hair behind her ears.

"I still think Logan has a point. The last note referred specifically to Laina and 'him', whichever one of us that is." Zach pushed his chair back with a scrape and gingerly stood.

"Where are you going?" Caroline asked as she placed mugs of coffee before Nick and Logan.

"To bed. I'm beat. I'll leave all this police work to you guys." He shuffled wearily to the doorway leading to the back hallway. "Sleep in either mom's or my room tonight Laina," he tossed over his shoulder. "And bring a bat."

Laina smiled to herself. "Some good you'll do fending off an intruder."

He waved in acknowledgment of her comment and disappeared down the hall. She shook her head and glanced at Logan. She was surprised to find him studying her intently.

She held her hands palm up. "What?"

"Mind if I take the couch?"

"I was kind of hoping you would. Those extra door and window locks you installed are great, but I'd feel a whole lot safer with my own personal body guard," she admitted with a relieved light in her blue eyes.

Logan's serious look broke with a cheeky wink. Laina's expression lit with amusement. Being loved by him in return was not something she had expected. She was thoroughly enjoying it, despite the circumstances.

"Come on guys, back to this list," Nick encouraged.

Caroline sat down with a mug for Laina and one for herself, and the brainstorming continued.

* * *

"We need to talk."

The sharp words and the familiar feminine voice gave Laina a start. Already feeling jumpy checking her e-mail while the receptionist was having a coffee break, she glanced up from the computer at the front desk at work.

Brylie was her usual stunning self in a red patterned halter neck top that complimented perfect curves. The outfit was completed with a knee length black satin skirt layered with chiffon. The word elegant came to Laina's mind. She wasn't surprised Zach had fallen for her. But how he hadn't seen past the beautiful exterior to the coldness beneath, she would never know.

Her pulse accelerated. Could Brylie truly have been the one who delivered last night's threat? Gary was out the back checking harnesses and the other rescue equipment, so Laina wasn't too worried about her safety. However, the bitterness in the other woman's brown eyes was still unnerving.

"About Zach?" Laina cut to the chase and held eye contact.

Gorgeous brunette curls styled to perfection brushed her shoulders as the other woman shrugged gently. The calm gesture belied the cool directness of her gaze. She nodded toward the front entrance.

"Let's take a short walk."

Laina squashed the overwhelming urge to be polite and obeyed Logan's wishes. "Here will have to do, Brylie. I got another threat last night, so I'd just as soon stay within shouting distance of my colleagues."

Surprise disarmed Brylie in an instant and some of the fire left her eyes. Laina had deliberately dropped that piece of information to gauge her reaction, and she was pleased she had.

"I'm sorry. Have the police figured out who is sending them?"

"No, this one was delivered in person. Nick sent it off to the crime lab to be analyzed." Laina clicked out of her inbox and pushed back from the desk.

The receptionist would be back soon. She gestured to a row of chairs against the plate glass window beside the entrance and moved to take a seat. Brylie took the invitation and sat next to her rival, positioned so they were face to face.

"I'm sorry about you and Zach," Laina attempted conciliatory conversation.

The cool draught returned.

"Are you?"

Laina stared into the other woman's resentful eyes and decided to be candid. "Look, Brylie, I know what you're thinking and quite frankly, I find your insinuation offensive. I also don't like the accusations you made to Zach about the two of us. I'm in love with Logan and we're engaged. And as for my brother, he is my biggest ally and couldn't be happier for us."

This piece of news took Brylie off guard and she floundered for a response. Laina did not allow her time.

"You're a beautiful woman Brylie, but you have serious insecurities that have not only ruined your relationship with my brother, but show a deeper spiritual problem that concerns me."

Brylie's eyes lit with anger and she opened her mouth with a cutting reply. Laina silenced her with a raised hand and an expression brooking no nonsense.

"I'm not finished!" Laina's gaze matched the other woman's for ferocity. "You've crossed the line. You came into my mother's home, looked down your nose at us all, treated me with disrespect, and have had the audacity to accuse my brother and I of... of... I don't know how to word what you've accused us of, but I know it feels offensive." Laina's temper cooled as swiftly as it had ignited.

Brylie had the good grace to look ashamed. She was intently studying the classy Prada bag clutched in her hands.

"Zach cares about you," Laina softened her approach. "We all do. That's why we're worried."

Brylie's gaze whipped up to meet Laina's in confusion. "Worried about me? There's nothing wrong with *me*."

"I think if you're honest, deep down you're feeling just as empty of God's love as Zach was." Laina held her gaze, her blue eyes gentle.

"I don't know what you're talking about." Brylie's chin rose in prideful opposition.

Laina's lips tugged ever so slightly with a knowing smile. "Oh I think you do."

Her brown irises narrowed angrily. "You are so full of yourself Laina Jackson!" She stood. "I don't know what Logan sees in a pious, conceited woman like you!"

Laina chose to ignore the verbal jab and leaned back casually in her chair, studying her.

"Zach ended the relationship with you because he felt God pulling him in another direction, one that would restore the closeness he once had with Jesus. If you were headed along that same path, then maybe he wouldn't have broken it off.

"Brylie, you care more for your designer labels and illustrious career than your eternity. That's what we're worried about."

Brylie was clearly highly affronted, and her tone said as much. "I'm a Christian too, Laina, just not a sanctimonious one."

Laina was reaching the limit of her patience. "If that's so, why is there only rustling leaves and no spiritual fruit on your branches?"

Brylie seethed. "You know nothing about me or my life!" She slashed the air with her hand.

"Maybe not," Laina acquiesced with a sigh. "But I know genuine love when I see it, and recognize when it's just not there. The only way for you to know how to truly love Zach, or any person for that matter, is to experience it at the Cross first for yourself. Then you'll know it's more than warm feelings, fanciful dreams and having control."

Brylie's eyes snapped with fury and she drew back her right arm. Laina was in no position to avoid the blow, so she braced herself. A masculine hand suddenly gripped Brylie's wrist as she reached forward to strike.

Both women's eyes swung to Gary. Where he had come from, neither of them knew. Judging by his expression, he was none too happy. Brylie wrenched her arm free and glared at him.

"Don't touch me!"

"It's time you left," Gary replied coldly and reached for the door handle close by. He pulled it open and waited.

Brylie cast Laina one last withering glare before leaving with head held high and high heels click-clacking on the floor. Gary closed the door decisively behind her and turned to Laina.

"Are you okay?"

Laina sighed and let her head fall back against the plate glass. "I'm sorry, Gaz. I let my temper get the best of me."

"I didn't think so," he answered mildly. "You weren't the one raising your hand and I didn't hear you say anything that wasn't true."

He sat beside her, his large presence and his friendship comforting.

"Thanks, I appreciate it." Laina turned her head to look at him and she frowned curiously. "Just how long were you standing there?"

Gary shrugged and stood. "I heard her raised voice all the way from the back room. I figured you'd bumped into a disgruntled customer."

Laina sighed and rose. "If only. She's my brother's ex."

"Why was she mad at *you*?"

Laina rolled her eyes. "It's a long story. You need any help back there?"

Gary smiled. "Sure. You can scrub down the inside of the chopper. It got a little messy early this morning and the changeover of shifts happened before someone could get to it."

Laina's look was dry. "I see you've saved the best job for me."

Gary preceded her past the front desk through a passageway. "As always."

Laina shook her head and followed her partner.

* * *

The reality of what Laina had said began to sink in. So that was how it was to be! Betrayal, hurt and bitter anger all vied for position. There was no way she should be allowed to get away with it. Not this time. She had been warned.

A plan began to formulate.

16

Laina absorbed Logan's suggestion and her eyes widened. His look was warm, albeit broken by a cheeky wink.

"A marriage license? Today?"

Logan's expression became solemn. "I was serious that night in the hospital about wanting to marry you."

He had collected her from work and driven her to a building in town she did not recognize. They were sitting in the parking lot in his truck.

A slow smile tugged at her lips and warmth lit her blue eyes. "Oh Logan, I love you."

Fire came alive in his green eyes, however he must have reminded himself of her earlier wishes, for he did not follow through and kiss her. "I love you too."

Laina studied his winsome face and a barrage of questions assaulted her stunned mind. "Do we need blood tests? Is there a waiting period? How does this work?"

He pointed to the building they were parked behind. "None of the above apply in Wyoming State. We just make an appointment with the County Clerk's Office in there and fill out an application. The license will be granted on the spot, and in case you've got cold feet, you can relax in the knowledge the license won't expire with time."

Laina was astonished as her mind made the connections. "You've made us an appointment for today?"

Logan grinned mischievously. "In five minutes."

She was flabbergasted. "When?"

"When what? When do you want to get married?"

"Yes."

He looked hopeful. "Sunday afternoon?"

Laina was surprised by the closeness of the date. That passed quickly with a thrill of excitement.

She grinned. "I'd best go shopping then, hey?"

He brushed her chin with a gentle finger, his warm smile communicating a depth of love and desire. "Get to it, Ace."

They exchanged warm smiles and got out of the vehicle. It was with a sense of rightness, and a small measure of amazement, that Laina walked with her fiancé hand in hand into the County Clerk's Office.

* * *

Caroline fingered another snow white gown on the rack and marveled at the beauty surrounding her. The small bridal boutique in Walkerville was packed with everything from shoes and jewelry, to all manner of material confection.

"Laina honey," Caroline asked gently, "are you sure you're doing this for the right reasons?"

Laina turned with a happy smile from browsing the opposite rack to her mother. "Mom, I love him. I have since we were teenagers."

Caroline met her gaze and could not have missed the peaceful contentment there. She relaxed. "And you're not just speeding things up because of the stalker and Vince Moretto?"

Laina stared pensively past the mannequin brides out the front window to the busy walkway. It was Saturday afternoon, and the pavement was getting a good workout.

"I'd be lying if I didn't admit I'll feel safer being with Logan all the time. When I think about it, coming home to him after every shift and never having to say goodnight, has been a dream I've had to bury for a long time. I'm really looking forward to having him in my life every day permanently. He's not just my best friend, Mom. He's my soul mate."

Caroline's eyes misted and she blinked back unexpected tears. She clasped Laina's upper arms and gave them a squeeze. "That's so beautiful, honey. I felt the same way about Zach's dad. I still do."

Laina heard the grief left unspoken and embraced her mother. Finally they parted and Laina busied herself perusing the gowns to give Caroline a moment to compose herself.

"I mean, don't get me wrong. I'm sure learning to live together will be tricky and we'll both have moments when we'll want to throttle each other, but I'd say that's pretty normal."

Caroline chuckled and went back to surveying layers of silk, satin and lace. "It is."

"As for knowing each other well enough for marriage... I can't think of a single topic we haven't covered during our friendship."

"I can think of one," Caroline remarked dryly.

Laina smiled to herself. "We're tackling that subject tonight. Pastor wanted to catch us for a counseling session before we say 'I do' tomorrow."

Caroline restrained an amused smile. "I'm glad to hear it. Money management is another good one to touch on. Oh, and make sure you both discuss personal views on the ideal roles you think a husband and wife should have. Subconscious expectations can be a killer."

"Making a mental note of it." Laina pushed aside ruffles and tulle to get a better look at the sparkle catching her eye nearby. She pulled the dress free from its competitors and let out a soft, "Wow!"

Caroline turned to see what had her interest and her face slowly lit with delight. "I think you've found it."

Laina beamed with excitement. "I most certainly have."

* * *

Zach struggled with his tie at the bathroom mirror. "Where are we going?"

His mother had been strangely cryptic all afternoon.

"Like I've already told you," Caroline reiterated from behind him, "we're going out and you need to look your best."

"I'm not really feeling up to going out. Can't we wait a few days?" He tugged at the ill formed knot at his throat.

"Just trust me, Zach. This is one surprise afternoon you're going to love." Caroline stepped in to assist with the tie.

Her eyes carried a pleased sparkle that Zach found intriguing. "Alright. You win."

She finished with the tie and gave his dark suit a quick perusal. "There, you look wonderful."

"Can you at least tell me where we'll be eating?"

"Who said we were going to dinner?" She breezed from the bathroom with a mischievous sparkle in her eyes.

Zach stared after her in bewilderment. He glanced at himself one more time in the mirror. He had black circles under his eyes and although he'd shaved, he looked a little gaunt. He turned away from the disturbing image and slowly followed his mother.

He hoped she was right about liking this surprise, because the call of his pillow was awfully loud at the moment.

✳ ✳ ✳

Zach was even more intrigued when Anne, Walter and Tia Mathews arrived at their front gate, also in their finest attire. He was gob smacked when Caroline invited them all to follow her into the woods on foot behind her home.

She wordlessly led the way on a small forest trail he and Laina had used when they were kids. Logan's family seemed as mystified as Zach was. Their quietly murmured questions echoed those in his own mind.

When Laina's uncle's abuse had caused her to reach her limit, she had moved into a little tree house high in an ancient oak. By the time Zach had met her a little over a year later, she had become self sufficient.

Zach could hear the creek rippling joyfully and knew the clearing and the tree house would come into view around the next bend.

However, neither he nor his companions were prepared for the sight that awaited them all. They rounded the last twist in the trail and the Mathews ground to a halt. Zach was just as stunned as they were. The clearing had been transformed.

He glanced at his mom and was not surprised to see that she looked extremely pleased. What was going on?

Six chairs covered neatly in white linen and wrapped with large gold bows stood slightly behind an arbor entwined with a variety of beautiful flowers. Three chairs to the right and three were to the left of an aisle of rose petals.

Beneath the arbor stood the pastor of the local church they all attended, dressed in a formal suit and holding an open Bible in his hands.

Off to the right was a table covered in a lovely lace

cloth, decorated by a bouquet of roses, baby's-breath and lilies. A gold pen sat atop a set of neatly arranged papers.

"Please be seated," Pastor Jacobs invited with a kind smile.

* * *

Now beginning to gain some understanding, the small gathering found their seats. Caroline and Zach took two to the left, and the Mathews' the three to the right. Tia busied herself with a rose bloom plucked from the arbor, while Walter had a quiet, but rather intense discussion with Anne. In uncharacteristic form, she hushed him with one sharp warning and a stern look.

Logan stepped into the clearing and approached the small group. Zach shook his head in amazement and passed his friend a cheeky grin.

"You sneaky little-"

"Sh!" Caroline gave him a playful nudge. "The groom has something he wants to say."

Walter and Anne exchanged glances and together stared at their son as he moved to stand before the group.

"I know this is probably a bit of a shock," Logan began nervously when he reached the front, "and I'm sure gossip will run rife about why we rushed things and eloped this way. But when all is said and done, each of you here are the ones who matter the most to us." He drew a steady breath.

"I've loved Laina for as long as I can remember, and she loves me." Logan's look was chagrined. "And unfortunately neither of us is great with crowds, so..." He gestured to the arbor and the seats. "Here we are."

Caroline laughed and Zach beamed. Anne's hands covered her mouth and tears of happiness clouded her vision. Walter was unreadable. A long look passed between father and son. Logan was unsure how his dad would take the announcement. The last thing anyone wanted was an ugly confrontation. Yet to deny him the chance to see his son marry seemed wrong.

Walter nodded and offered his hand. Logan hid his surprise and stepped forward to shake it. He resumed his place before the pastor, who leaned down to switch on a battery operated stereo. Pachelbel's Canon filled the still afternoon air and everyone automatically twisted in their chairs to see the trail behind them.

Long seconds ticked by, and finally Laina appeared.

Her long blond hair had been curled and gently pulled back at the sides with a small, glittering tiara. Two broad triangles of gathered chiffon formed straps over milky white shoulders. Sheer fabric gathered atop satin across the bust, met at a central delicate silver clasp, accentuating a lovely shape.

Bejeweled lace sparkled on the bodice of her snow white gown, set alight by the sun filtering down through the canopy of leaves above them. The fitted satin skirt shone beneath a thin layer of sparsely patterned lace, flowing elegantly to the forest floor and finishing in glimmering scalloped edges. A modest train lightly brushed the grass.

Stylish silver shoes peeked from beneath the gown upon a carpet of scattered rose petals as Laina walked serenely in the direction of the groom.

Logan was entranced. He didn't know how he had imagined his bride would look, but nothing like the stunning beauty coming toward him. He swallowed hard and quickly blinked back tears. He had waited so long, and now she was finally about to become his.

* * *

Laina's gaze encompassed Logan's family, her mother's big smile, and then her brother. Unsure what his reaction would be, she was thrilled to see only happiness in his expression. Zach wagged a finger at her. Laina subtly shrugged and sent him a happy smile. He grinned.

Her gaze turned to the man she was about to marry. The love and wonder in his eyes stole her breath away. Logan's countenance was as open as she had ever seen it, and she drank in all he was communicating.

As she came to stand before the pastor and Logan took her hands in his, a small part of her heart ached for her father to be here to give her away. She was saddened that Uncle Rylan had been unexpectedly out of town with his wife on business. He was scheduled to come back in a day or two.

As she prepared to take Logan as her husband, a comforting thought entered her mind and soothed her aching heart. Surely her dad was looking down from heaven.

* * *

After signing their marriage certificate, Logan and Laina posed for photographs with their family. The pastor's wife, Patricia Jacobs, had unobtrusively slipped into the third seat beside Zach after the bride's entrance, carrying a camera. She took enough pictures to fill several albums and finally cleared the table and disappeared down the trail.

The group mingled and enjoyed talking, unsuspecting of the next surprise. Patricia arrived, followed by her two teenage daughters bearing trays of delicious savory and sweet treats. One final trip produced drinks and a simple, but elegantly decorated wedding cake.

The setting sun cast its golden glow over the bride and groom as they cut the cake and shared their first meal with their family as husband and wife.

It was a day they knew they would never forget.

* * *

Logan slid the deadbolt in place and turned to his bride standing in the living room behind him.

Laina's mind replayed the terrifying scene ending with her injured on the floor and Vince's blood on her polished boards. The blood was gone and the house was now spotless, but the memories were still very much alive.

"Are you sure no one can get in?" Her uncertain gaze met his and compassion filled his countenance.

"I'm sure, Ace. I've tightened the security, installed an alarm system, and even added locks to the windows. Short of building in steel bars, this place is as safe as it can get."

Laina nodded, her line of vision going involuntarily to where she had lain. Logan crossed the short distance between them. He took her hands in his and bent his head to catch her gaze.

"No one's getting past me, Ace. No one. You're safe."

Laina searched his eyes and was satisfied with what she found. Her anxiety abated and she relaxed.

"Thanks Logan."

He draped an arm around her shoulders and allowed his eyes to wander the open living space. They had both agreed that since Laina owned her house thanks to her dad's inheritance, that this would be their home. Logan looked pleased. He apparently liked his wife's taste in décor.

His wife. Laina let that new reality sink in as she slid an arm around the tall, muscular man at her side. She found him entirely appealing.

He gave her shoulders a gentle squeeze. "We'll make new memories here."

Laina smiled and looked up into his handsome face. "We will, starting with this." She reached up on tiptoe and rested a hand against his cheek, and sought his lips with hers.

Laina loved the feel of him beneath her fingers. He drew her against him and leaned into the kiss. It was sweet and inviting.

Their lips parted and the couple studied one another for several delighted seconds. Logan smiled blissfully and Laina could not help a grin of her own.

"Wow!"

"My thoughts exactly." Laina gently drew his head down for another.

The silence in the house lengthened as their love was finally able to find expression.

17

A loud knock on the door awoke the newlyweds early the next morning. Logan roused instantly and pulled on a pair of jeans from the suitcase on the floor. They would have to move the rest of his belongings in the next few days and rearrange things.

Laina sat up and blinked sleepily. She watched her husband retrieve a baseball bat from beneath the bed, not even realizing he had hidden it there. He had to have deposited it while leaving his suitcase the previous morning.

Logan's gaze passed over her in her satin nightgown and a saucy smile tugged at his lips. Laina automatically pulled the covers a little higher, unable to help the blush stealing up her neck. He winked and opened the bedroom door.

"Stay here till I know who it is," he instructed, the mischief in his eyes vanishing.

He slipped out the door and closed it behind him. Laina quickly tossed back the covers and threw on some clothes. She was not about to leave Logan alone at the front line of defense.

* * *

Logan peered out the new peephole in the front door. Seeing Nick in his deputy uniform, he relaxed and laid aside the bat. He opened the door and ran a hand through his hair, which had to be standing on end.

"Don't you ever sleep?" he greeted with a rusty voice.

Nick's brows lifted in surprise. Clearly he had not expected to find his best friend in Laina's house. The woman herself came into the living room in the next moment brandishing a tennis racket. Nick leaned around Logan to get a better view. She too still looked sleepy. His mind seemed to be putting two and two together and he did not look pleased with the conclusion.

"Oh Nick, it's only you." Laina sighed with relief and leaned against the arm of the couch. She tossed the bat on the cushions and rubbed scratchy eyes. She exhaled slowly. "Come on in. Have you had breakfast?"

Laina completely missed the troubled look on their friend's face as she wandered to the kitchen to boil the kettle. However, Logan saw the concern chasing across the deputy's countenance and resisted a mischievous smile.

He grabbed Nick by the arm and pulled him inside, firmly closing the door behind him. "What brings you to our neck of the woods?"

Logan brushed by his friend and headed to the kitchen. He wrapped his arms around Laina from behind as she withdrew mugs from a cupboard above the kettle, and planted a kiss atop her unruly blond hair. She smiled, sat the mugs on the counter and turned in his embrace to receive a morning kiss. She drew back from the brief contact and finally noticed the expression on their mutual friend's face.

Logan kept her close, resting his chin on the crown of her head and smiling with great amusement. Laina stifled a laugh.

She chuckled and flashed her left hand. "Nick, it's not what you think."

The gold band on her ring finger sparkled in the morning sun pouring through the living room windows. Nick caught its gleam and his jaw dropped. Astonishment replaced concern.

"You two got hitched? When?"

Logan's eyes glimmered cheekily. "Yesterday."

"You eloped?"

The couple grinned back at him.

"Sort of," Laina answered for them both. "And you're just in time to receive your invite to our celebration gathering at Gracie's tonight. You can help spread the word."

"Oh wow! This is… That's just… Oh wow!" Lost for words, Nick crossed the space between them and embraced Laina first and then Logan.

He stepped back, face beaming.

"Sit down." Logan gestured to one of the bar stools on the other side of the counter.

Laina reciprocated the smile. "Yeah, I'll whip up some pancakes while we tell you all about it."

Between the couple's explanation of the lead up to their rather sudden marriage and description of the blessed event itself, Nick peppered them with questions.

Finally pancakes started landing on plates, toppings were brought out and coffee was served. They shifted to the dining table and were heartily tucking into breakfast when Logan noticed a slight change in Nick's demeanor. Something was bothering him.

"So, how'd you end up on our doorstep at six in the morning?"

"I drive by Laina's when I can to keep an eye on things. When I saw her car in the driveway I was worried."

Logan studied his friend and concluded there was more. Nick forked in his last mouthful, took his time chewing, and then sipped his coffee before answering. Logan noted the stall tactics and his eyes narrowed.

"The stalker, right? You've found something."

Nick sighed and leaned back in his chair. "No, and that's the problem."

Laina pushed aside her plate, suddenly no longer hungry.

"The blood was from an animal. The paper used for the note was standard stock. The letters, however, were from a local newspaper. But still, thousands of people read it. A partial print was left on the scalpel, but no matches were found on state or national databases." Nick threw up his hands.

"So we're back where we started," Logan summarized.

Nick nodded, looking weary and dejected. Laina wasn't sure how she felt. All the same, she didn't want the people around her bearing such a heavy load because of her.

"We're still praying you'll find out who this guys is, Nick. God will come through. He always does. And I've got Him and the lot of you to keep me safe in the meantime. It'll be okay."

Nick smiled gratefully. His vision, like hers, was often taken up by the uglier side of humanity. She figured it was always good to be reminded of the One they should be gazing upon.

"You're right." He pushed away from the table and stood. "Anyway, I'd better get to work."

Logan gathered plates and mugs and took them to the sink while Laina saw their friend to the door.

"Hey don't forget, Gracie's tonight at six." She grinned happily.

Nick turned on the porch and smiled warmly. "I'll spread the word. And once Em get's wind of this, the whole town will show up."

Laina cringed. "Maybe don't spread the word to absolutely everyone. We eloped because we're not big on crowds."

Nick shrugged and a cheeky gleam entered his eyes. "You know small town life, Laina. There was no way you two were going to get away without some kind of over-the-top shindig."

Laina bit her bottom lip. "I was afraid of that."

Nick laughed and turned to his car behind hers in the driveway. He waved and got in. Laina shook her head and closed the door. She watched Logan who was busy at the kitchen sink.

"You do dishes too?"

Logan glanced up at her and smiled cheekily. "I even know how to put the toilet seat down."

Laina laughed. She moved to join him in the kitchen and the dishes were momentarily forgotten.

* * *

"We've all been keepin' our eyes on the two o' you for years. It was only a matter of time. The when and where, well, that was anyone's guess," Gracie acknowledged. "It's been a beautiful romance to watch." She raised her soda. "To the bride and groom!"

The crowd cheered and soda bottles clinked for the toast to the newlyweds. Gracie's café was packed with family and friends who had gathered to celebrate the nuptials of Logan and Laina Mathews.

Laina could hardly believe that together they knew so many people. Every seat and barstool was taken, leaving standing room only, and there wasn't much left of that.

"Talk about sneaky!" Nick declared.

"We want pictures!" Emily demanded with a grin beside him.

A chorus of agreement rippled through the gathering.

"I'll go you one better," Patricia Jacobs called as she tinkered with the television hanging on the wall at the end of the front counter. "Our daughters hid in the bushes nearby and took a video."

Laina's mouth dropped and she exchanged surprised glances with Logan. He chuckled and shook his head.

"We knew everyone would want to see these two shy lovebirds tie the knot," Pastor Jacobs teased.

Laughter filled the room as the DVD began.

"Hey, crank it up?" Zach shouted over the din. He was sitting with Wil Genner and the two had been catching up. Caroline was jammed between church friends in the next booth.

Patricia set the volume on high and the room quieted enough for the ceremony to be heard above the chatter and banter of the happy group.

An arm slipped around Laina's shoulders and she glanced up and to her right. Sparkling blue eyes, almost identical to her father's, smiled down at her.

Her face lit with excitement and she flung her arms around her uncle Rylan. He hugged her in return and then held her at arm's length.

"What is this?" he teased with a grin. "Jade and I go away for a couple of days and suddenly you're married."

Laina bit her lower lip, unable to restrain her smile. "You would have been invited if you'd been around."

"What's with the rush?"

Logan grinned and shook his hand. "What rush?

We've known each other for over ten years."

Rylan laughed softly. "Congratulations."

Logan responded with a smile. "Thanks."

The change in Laina's uncle was even more amazing than in Logan's life. Their conversions had been within the same week, ten years ago. However, Rylan Jackson had had to overcome serious anger management issues and put the pieces of his life back together again after his niece had been removed from his custody. He had married Jade quite a few years later and the two seemed perfectly suited.

"Hey, where's *my* hug?" she complained good-naturedly from his side.

Laina beamed and received another embrace. She liked her aunt immensely.

She stepped back. "Congrats, Laina! I'm so sorry we couldn't be there!"

Laina waved it aside. "You didn't know." She glanced at Logan and grinned. "Neither did we for that matter."

Jade's fingers covered her mouth. "That's so romantic! An elopement. You know I-"

"Sh gorgeous!" Rylan draped his arm around her shoulders and pointed to the T.V above the counter. "You're missing it."

Jade grinned at Laina who beamed in return. Logan was sitting on a barstool, and pulled her into his arms to watch. When the ceremony concluded and the groom kissed his bride, an irreverent shout nearly raised the rafters of the diner.

Congratulatory shouts and cheeky ribbing followed.

It set the scene for a wonderful evening of fun and laughter.

* * *

"That was a great party last night, Laina," Nate commented with his usual sparkling eyes the next morning. "Everyone out there is still talking about it."

He breezed into his office and tossed his wallet and keys onto the desk Laina was sitting behind. She clicked through her work e-mail and passed him a grin.

"It was, wasn't it? I don't know why we were so terrified of having a crowd in the first place."

He dropped into the chair opposite the one his co-worker was occupying.

"You know, one of these days we'll have to get a computer for you medics and stick it on a desk out in the staffroom or something." He noted with apparent amusement the familiarity with which his young friend used his office.

"The sooner the better." Laina opened an e-mail from Nick. "I'll be out of here in a second."

Nate studied her and smiled warmly. "Laina?"

"Yeah?" She glanced up from the screen and across the desk between them.

"Congratulations. I'm really proud of who and what you've become."

Laina held his gaze and her spirit lifted. He had not only saved her life as a teen, but had mentored her

169

through college and helped her to get the job she was in. "Thanks Nate. That means a lot coming from you."

He grinned. "You're welcome. Now get out of my chair."

He stood and circled the desk as Laina hastily read the message from Nick. She felt a stone sink to the bottom of her stomach and it began to churn.

'Enjoy married bliss while you can, because your days are numbered.'

"Oh no you don't!" she muttered angrily and immediately picked up the phone.

"Is it another threat?" Nate frowned and bent to read the screen. His gaze narrowed dangerously as he scanned the missive.

Meanwhile Laina dialed Zach's mobile. He picked up on the fourth ring.

"Hello?"

She wasted no time. "Zach, the stalker just sent me another e-mail this morning. This time it's from Nick's address. I need you to trace it. I'm forwarding it now."

"Okay, I'm getting my laptop. Where are you?"

"I'm at work. Nate is here."

"Alright. Stay close to him or Gary today. I'll get onto Nick and hunt this guy down."

Laina's eyes remained on the message. This was a distinct death threat. Tears blurred her vision and she blinked them back.

She took a deep breath. *Be an oak.*

Zach must have read her mood in the ensuing silence. "We'll find him, Laina."

She steadied her voice. "I know. Today would be good."

"By God's grace, I will."

"Thanks Zach," she replied softly and hung up.

Nate rested a hand on her shoulder. "You go prep for callouts with Gary and I'll deal with this."

Laina pushed the chair back and stood. She felt shaky. "I can't wait till this thing is over." She strode to the door.

"Don't worry, Laina, we'll catch this guy."

She turned in the doorway and met his compassionate gaze. She offered a weak smile and left as her boss was picking up the phone again to call the local sheriff's office.

18

Zach was stunned when the IP address he finally traced was different from the others. It had also been relatively easy to access. The miscreant had made a major mistake. Zach frowned. It was possible the stalker's mental stability was slipping, and therefore so was his caution. That could mean only one thing. He would carry through on his threat soon.

Zach dialed Nick on his mom's home phone.

They had a location and now a name. Oddly enough, it was female.

* * *

Laina navigated the ambulance along the narrow trail to a gravel parking area. It wasn't terribly far from Walkerville and the hiking trail made accessing the injured hiker relatively easy. Albeit, carrying the woman out would be difficult, but nothing they hadn't done before.

Laina set the park brake and turned off the engine. Gary was out of the vehicle instantly gathering gear. Laina was right behind him. He passed her the medical pack and he took the climbing gear and stretcher.

172

"Which trail?"

Laina pointed to their right where a rough hewn pathway led into the trees. She had walked it with Logan, Nick, Emily and Wil a few months ago.

"The dispatcher said it was the five mile trail along the top of the bluff."

"Should be fun carrying her back," Gary commented dryly.

Laina grinned. "You're the one who made the call to go by ambulance, not by chopper."

"Needed the exercise," he quipped in an unusually subdued mood, and started toward the woods.

* * *

Nick knocked on the front door of a small bungalow in a rundown section of Walkerville. His fellow deputy, Evan Miles, was at his side. The rookie was even greener than Nick. He had been on the job a total of thirty-five days. His wiry frame was tense, as though he expected the stalker to be on the other side of the door.

"No one's answering. Do we bust it down?"

Nick exhaled a longsuffering breath. "Not unless you want to explain trespassing without a warrant to the prosecuting judge."

"How long till the warrant comes through?"

"Too long for my liking. Charlie's working on it." Nick knocked again.

Finally light footsteps sounded on the other side and

aged hinges groaned as it opened. A woman in her late forties, dark hair and rather easy on the eyes, stared at them in surprise.

"Oh, hi." She opened the door wider.

"Ms Finlay?" Nick flashed his badge.

"Yes, how can I help you?"

"I'm Deputy Foster, and this is Deputy Miles. May we speak with you for a few minutes?"

Looking more curious than alarmed, the woman stepped aside to allow the men entrance. "Sure, come in and take a seat."

* * *

Zach waited patiently in the squad car by the curb. This was one conversation he was loathed to not be party to. He re-read the e-mail to his sister on his laptop open on his knee. This sounded more like a jealous male, not a sixteen-year-old girl.

Seraya Finlay owned the computer that had sent the message. Zach wished he were a fly on the wall as Nick spoke with the girl's mother. He didn't have long to wait.

Nick reemerged at a jog not five minutes later, Evan hot on his heels. They climbed into the car, Nick behind the wheel. In seconds the lights and siren were on and the vehicle was moving toward downtown Walkerville.

"Nick, what it is? What did she say?" Alarm notched up Zach's heart rate as the car swerved and pushed

174

him against the passenger door. He grimaced and clutched his side.

Nick's mouth was set in a grim line. He took another corner sharply and accelerated. He explained as he forced his way through busy lunchtime traffic.

"Finlay is Debbie's maiden name, which she kept when she got married eighteen years ago. Her ex-husband was over this morning to take their daughter to school."

"So you think he's the stalker? How does he connect with Laina?"

"Zach, the girl's father is Gary Wilson."

Spots danced across Zach's vision as shock slammed into him. No, it couldn't be! He felt sick with the knowledge he had encouraged his sister to stay close to the very man that was obsessed with her.

Evan was already calling in the information via dispatch while Nick raced towards the EMT home office. Zach dialed his sister's mobile from the back seat. After several unsuccessful tries, he called Logan, dreading what he had to tell his brother-in-law.

* * *

Laina pointed ahead. "It should be just past the bluff here, going by what the dispatcher said."

To the left, forest and shrubbery wound back into the wild, green countryside. To their right, the rocky trail dropped away dramatically into a valley filled with all manner of native trees. At the bottom of the bluff a small creek trickled across rocky ground into the surrounding forest. Although hastening along the trail, Laina found herself enjoying the outdoors immensely.

"I can't believe we get paid to do this job." She flashed a grin at her partner behind her.

Gary's sour expression caused her steps to falter and she frowned in bewilderment.

"What's the matter?" Her focus returned to the rocky pathway at her feet. They needed to make good time. Every minute counted. She didn't want the hiker going into shock.

"You just had to, didn't you?" His unexpected words were a bitter snarl.

Laina started to turn, but not before two strong hands grabbed her pack and pulled her to an abrupt stop.

"Do the words 'Enjoy married bliss while you can, because your days are numbered,' ring a bell?" Gary's words breathed softly in her ear, sent alarm bells jangling in Laina's consciousness.

Before she had time to react, hands powered by rage propelled her to the bluff. She tumbled at first and then let loose a terrified cry as she slid straight over the edge. The drop was not immediate.

She was slipping, rolling, careening out of control. Skin tore on sharp pieces of rock. Jagged edges bumped and bruised. Her mind screamed for it to stop. She kept falling. Suddenly the bluff fell away and gravity pulled at her feet, drawing her downward.

The pack caught on a protruding rock and Laina was jarred to a halt. She stopped screaming. Each breath came ragged and in a gasp. Fifty yards below her, rugged terrain waited impatiently for impact and certain death.

She glanced up. She could see only the ledge she had fallen over. It inclined inward below her but seemed to be in reach. She couldn't go up. So that left going down.

Laina forced herself to calm down and think logically. An ominous tearing sound filled her overwrought senses. A burst of panic stole her breath away. The pack wasn't going to hold for much longer. She had to get her hands on that rock wall and fast!

Please God, help me? Keep me safe for Logan's sake, and my family's?

She un-clicked the waist clip and gripped the right strap. She carefully twisted her left arm, slipping free. Her right shoulder came clear with a jolt and the pack above her tore further. She had seconds.

Dangling from the final strap, she twisted and gently reached for the wall behind her. Her fingers found a good handhold. They slipped and she swung outward. She had no chalk powder to eliminate the sweat on her hands.

Laina gritted her teeth in frustration and very real fear. She swung in and tried again. Success! Letting go of the pack, she grabbed at the same jagged rock with her right hand. Her forearms protested as they held her weight while she searched blindly for a foothold.

There, that was sturdy. Her right foot found an outcrop just below her knees. Her left joined the right. Okay, she was balanced.

She exhaled in relief and glanced around for a climbable pathway. Without allowing herself to look down, Laina began her decent. One wrong move and it would all be over.

* * *

With his heart in his throat, Logan gunned the throttle and tore down the dirt track behind Nick's patrol car. Another squad car was catching up behind him.

Logan had raced to the EMT headquarters after Zach's call, only to find his friends exiting the building at a run. With a hurried explanation from Nick, they headed for the hiking trails outside of Walkerville.

The parking lot came into view. Nick jammed on his brakes and the tires skidded to a stop. Logan pulled up behind him in the resulting cloud of dust. He climbed from the truck and met with Nick, Evan and Zach. The second squad car parked and the two Walkerville officers joined the group.

"Okay, here's how this is going down. We don't want Gary getting spooked by all these uniforms and trying something." He began to outline a plan of action.

* * *

She was only twenty yards from the bottom of the bluff. Suddenly a rope dropped down beside her, uncoiling its way to the ground below. Her heart seized with dread. He was coming after her. The movement of the rope showed he was now repelling down.

She could use the rope to slide to the bottom. What if he cut it when he felt her weight? No, he wanted her. He knew he had to reach the base of the bluff to finish what he had begun. Laina thought quickly. Repelling down the cliff face would be easy and take only seconds. When he reached her, she was a dead woman.

She got hold of the rope with her right hand. With it firmly in her grasp, she thrust her left into her EMT jacket pocket and gripped the line through the thick fabric. She let go her right and grasped the material over her other hand for security. Holding her breath, she slid down the rope at a rapid pace. Two yards from the bottom, she tightened her grip to slow her decent. She hit the ground running.

Gary cursed from further up the bluff. Laina did not turn around or glance back. Every part of her ached from her slide over the ledge, but she did not slow down. She raced over rocky ground to the creek and cleared it in one leap. She landed badly and stumbled to her knees. Only then did she dare look over her shoulder. He was coming. He had reached the bottom and was unclipping his harness from the rope.

Gary tossed the rope aside with an impatient thrust and started after her at a sprint. Laina pulled herself to her feet and ran for the trees. She ducked a low branch and pushed through shrubbery, making her way further into the woods. Her lungs were burning. She had to get help, but that was simply not possible from the base of the bluff.

What if she climbed back up and ran to the ambulance? She could lock herself in it and use the radio. Gary was a fast climber. Could she out-climb him? She had to, or he would find her and then... She shuddered. She couldn't give up. She *wouldn't* give up.

Laina completed a tear in her jacket and hooked the material over a twig in the opposite direction to the one she intended to take back to the bluff. She then moved on silent feet, just as Logan had taught her when she was a teenager, back toward Gary. She ducked out of sight within some shrubbery and waited, willing her breathing to slow.

Twigs snapped and leaves crunched beneath swift footfalls. She could hear his rapid breathing even before he came into view. She held completely still and prayed he wouldn't find her. She was counting on his haste to cause him to miss the details, such as imprints in the grass, and the absence of the sound of her own retreat.

Laina held her breath as he rushed by not two paces from where she was hiding. She released it when he kept going. She saw him pause and take the torn fabric from the twig and then continue. She waited. An agonizing minute ticked by. The sound of footfalls continued and he disappeared from sight.

Laina came out of her hiding place and started back

for the bluff as swiftly and silently as she could manage. She reached the clearing and ran for the creek. One leap. She landed on good footing and made for the bluff.

She heard Gary yelling but did not stop to listen to the words he was saying. She chose an easier patch of rock to climb that lifted straight toward the sky, rather than the inverse section she had descended.

Gary's voice was drawing closer. Laina chanced a glance over her shoulder as she started up. Her heart leapt into her throat. He had realized she'd doubled back and was now at the edge of the woods. She hastened her movements, frantically searching for good holds and solid footing. She could not afford to falter. It would be her death.

She estimated she had to be five yards up.

"You little..." Gary's words trailed off as he reached the bottom of the bluff and began climbing after her.

Fear constricted her chest and she gulped back tears, reaching for the next hold, the next step up. She had to win this time. She just had to!

"Why are you doing this?" She continued her desperate effort to escape.

His labored breathing drew nearer. His legs were longer, his reach further than hers. It had always been his advantage.

"Because I hate you! You were mine, rightfully mine! Things were good, and they were only going to get better. Then you betrayed me," he verbally spat the words. "You lied and said you weren't dating Logan, but you were. You could have apologized. I would have forgiven you. But you went ahead heartlessly and married him!" Gary's explanation ended in an angry explosion. He was steadily gaining on her.

His words were like a knife. *Father, he's delusional! He's lost his mind. Save me from this maniac?*

"Don't say I didn't warn you!"

He spoke from directly below her, and he sounded dangerously calm. Laina gulped back panic and reached for the next hold above her.

Fingers latched onto her ankle and she felt an almighty tug. Her grip loosened and she felt herself falling. He let go of her.

Laina grabbed at Gary as she fell. Her fingers failed to grip his jacket, but slid to the belt at his waist and held on. He lost his balance as her full weight pulled him with her. She let go as soon as he began falling. Several terrifying seconds later her feet connected with smooth ground.

Laina rolled to take the pressure from her legs upon impact. She tumbled over more rocky ground and finally lay still. She was hurting, really hurting. And as she looked over at Gary five feet away, she realized the pain was in more ways than one.

19

Logan spotted the rope anchored to a tree and followed it to the ledge. According to Nick, the hiker was
supposed to be further up the trail. Why had someone
repelled down the bluff, and where was the spotter for
the one abseiling?

His heart plummeted in dread. They were too late.

"Nick, you better get over here!" He peered over the
bluff.

Feet pounded the dirt and Nick, Evan and the two
back up officers materialized at his side. Zach had
needed to take a slower pace to walk in. He wouldn't
be too far behind.

Logan saw Gary sprawled face down at the base
of the bluff, and close by was Laina. She was lying on
her side with her knees drawn up to her chest, facing
her partner. Neither figure moved. Logan ran anxious
hands through his hair and debated what to do.

"Laina, are you alright?"

"Laina, answer us! Are you okay?" Nick tried.

She did not respond, did not even glance up. Logan
was done messing around. He removed his sweater
and wrapped his right hand. He grasped the rope with
the wad of material and curled the end around himself,

feeding it through his left.

"You're not doing what I think you're doing," Nick protested mildly.

"She's not okay. Don't expect me to stand by up here and wait. I won't do it." Logan's determined gaze met Nick's.

Nick shook his head in defeat, knowing a losing battle when he encountered one. "At least let me dig up a harness from the back of the ambulance?"

"We're wasting precious time. Call Nate and have a couple of these guys go fetch that hiker." Logan backed over the edge, supporting his weight with the rope.

"Who's in charge here?" Nick leveled him with a dry look as he disappeared.

* * *

Logan dropped the last few feet and discarded his sweater, now worn through where the rope had been. He assessed the scene more closely and felt sick to his stomach. Gary had hit the side of his head upon impact. Logan didn't know how far he had fallen, but it had been high enough that the man had not survived.

He quickly focused upon his wife, crossing the short distance between them and crouching down in front of her. She was conscious, for which he was immensely grateful. However, something was seriously wrong. She was violently shaking.

"Ace, talk to me. Where are you hurt?"

She flinched at the touch of his hand on her shoulder. He kept it there, gentle but firm. Shattered eyes met his and she seemed to finally realize who she was staring at.

"It was him. Logan, it was Gary."

Logan's heart clenched painfully. "I know. I'm so sorry, Laina. We just found out."

Her gaze rested upon her partner. Logan positioned himself between her and the upsetting sight. She still looked vacant and it scared him. He helped her into a sitting position and ran his hands along her arms and legs checking for breaks or bleeding. He noted in alarm that she was ice cold. She was sliding further and further into shock, and if something wasn't done, she would die.

"Nick, how long till Nate gets here?" he shouted to his friend at the top of the bluff.

Nick suddenly appeared over the edge, wearing a harness he had no doubt appropriated from Laina and Gary's supplies. He began to repel down the rock wall.

"Is she badly hurt?"

"Some grazing and a few gashes, but nothing seems to be broken. It's the shock I'm worried about." Logan went to retrieve his sweater.

He would add another layer of clothing and hope it helped raise her temperature, which had dropped dangerously from lack of proper circulation.

Nick reached the ground as Logan was threading the sweater over Laina's head. She was no longer responding to any of his attempts at conversation. It was like she had slipped into another world. Post traumatic stress? Concussion?

Nick knelt by Gary's side and felt for a pulse. He met Logan's gaze and shook his head gravely. He joined his friends.

"Nate was on standby when we left. I called him after you went over the edge. He'll be only a minute or two away." Nick observed Laina's colorless features.

Logan wrapped his arms around her and felt broken to see silent tears streaming down her cheeks. At least she was reacting in some way to her situation, but it hurt so much to see her in pain.

* * *

Calvin Benton paused at the new HP model computer on display and smiled. The 'my videos' tab was open and a couple of teenagers' faces stared back at him from a webcam shot they had taken of themselves.

He needed to get ink for his home printer, but he did enjoy looking at the newer model computers coming out. His wife was shopping in the store next door. Knowing her 'five' minute browsing, he had at least another fifteen minutes before he needed to meet her at the car. For the sake of curiosity, he pressed play.

The clip was amusing and he chuckled at their antics. He was about to hit delete when something in the background caught his eye. He replayed it. This time he froze the frame and zoomed in on the image that had captured his attention.

Calvin frowned and studied the man behind the teens along the row of computers on display opposite them. What was he doing? And that face... It was familiar. Then it dawned on him.

Work! He had seen this guy at the Walkerville County Police building where he worked as a janitor. The picture was tacked up on a whiteboard surrounded by sticky notes regarding a case and diagrams connecting events, people and places. This was Vince Moretto! And judging by the time indicated on the video clip, he had been in this shop not more than ten minutes ago.

Calvin withdrew his cell phone from his pocket and dialed his workplace.

* * *

"No, I'm not spending a night in hospital!" Laina declared vehemently.

Logan's gaze narrowed and they faced one another stubbornly. Laina was sitting on the edge of a gurney, and Logan was blocking her path of escape. Zach watched the standoff with a raised brow from a nearby chair.

"Young love."

The remark got him glared at by the bickering couple. He rose and made a hasty retreat.

"I think I'll just wait in the car."

"Good call," Logan replied dryly.

"I'm coming with you." Laina slipped past him and he caught her gently by the arm.

"Two hours ago we were close to losing you from shock. Laina, please? Just humor me?" he pleaded softly.

"That's the point, Logan." She averted her gaze. "I'm not alright. The physical effects of today have worn off, but inside I'm struggling and I really need to be home with you, not in hospital where that smell reminds me of every traumatic moment I've had in my life."

Logan remembered those moments she was referring to. She had lost her dad, and several years later been abducted and suffered resulting injuries. He couldn't find it in his heart to argue.

"Okay." He drew her into an embrace.

Laina hugged him in return. This was what she needed, not more medical staff intruding into her thoughts.

"Come on, Ace." He released her and held her hand as they exited the curtained off area. "Your mom's gonna kill me, but you can have it your way tonight. I reckon you've earned it." He passed her a sideways smile.

She returned it with a rueful one of her own.

* * *

"Thanks for everything Nate," Logan spoke into his cell phone quietly from beside his wife in bed.

She was curled up on the pillow next to his, her eyes

puffy and her cheeks blotchy. She had cried herself to sleep fifteen minutes ago. All he'd been able to do was hold her and pray, but it seemed to have been enough. She was sleeping peacefully now.

"Tell her I don't want to see her darken the doorway any time soon," Nate instructed.

"Oh I will. I think we'll take a nice long honeymoon."

"You do that. I'll talk to you in a few weeks."

With that, Nate disconnected the line and Logan placed his cell on the nightstand. He turned off the lamp beside their bed and wrapped his arms around his wife once again. Sleep was not far away.

* * *

Deputy Brian Smith studied a map of the county pinned to a board on the wall of the Walkerville Sheriff's Office. Markings indicated where patrol cars were stationed, creating roads blocks within a fifty mile radius. Other officers moved around him while he silently mused. His brows were furrowed in thought.

Eyewitness accounts from shoppers put Vince in a nearby convenience store after the computer shop, where he had used a stolen credit card to purchase food. So far there had been no more activity on the card.

The storekeeper had seen him leave in an old model white Dodge. In a twist of good fortune, Vince had parked near the bank next door. Having his rough time of departure, Brian had been able to use security footage from the bank camera covering the ATM and sidewalk area, to pick up a plate number from his car as he drove away. The plates too were fake, however it had at least given authorities enough to issue a BOLO alert on the vehicle and set up a perimeter with road blocks.

It had been too long. He should have been spotted by now. Brian exhaled loudly and shook his head. Somehow he had slipped through.

"Brian," a voice called to his right.

Deputy Watkins stood at his desk, phone to his ear and the receiver covered with his free hand. "I've got a rancher on the line who lives down near Whistler Creek. He says there's a car in the ditch by the entrance to his property. It's a white Dodge."

Brian's heart sank. "Number plate?"

Watkins conversed briefly with the rancher and turned again to respond. He covered the receiver, his eyes losing their glimmer. "It a match. The car is empty and has a buckled fender. There are no signs of injury. It's just been abandoned."

Brian's gaze returned to the map and he marked the spot mentioned with a red X. "Thank the man and tell him we'll be out shortly to look it over."

Deputy Watkins complied and hung up. He joined Brian at the board.

"My guess is he crashed the vehicle into the ditch intentionally and hitched a ride with some softhearted local who came to his aid," the deputy surmised grimly.

Brian nodded slowly. "My thoughts too. It was likely

stolen in the first place and would only draw attention the further he drove it. Alright people," he called over the din in the room, "our fugitive has breached the blockade. We've lost our most solid lead. Keep a tight watch on that credit card, and please tell me you've found somebody who can trace the e-mail Vince sent from the computer store?"

"Still no activity on the card," Deputy Calloway replied.

"Our computer guys are all out of town. One is on vacation overseas, another at a conference interstate and the last just got off a 24 hour all nighter. You could try the next county over, or you could speak with Nick Foster over in Icy Creek? He's got a friend who's a computer whizz. The guy helped us track down a stalker today," Watkins suggested.

It had been just before the changeover of shifts that afternoon, and the men that had attended the scene had debriefed the office of the day's events.

"Get me his name and number immediately," Brian demanded. "Let's find out who Vince e-mailed before he skipped town. It might be just the lead we need to catch this guy before his trail goes cold."

* * *

Zach rubbed bleary eyes and sat his mobile on his bedside table. So much for this being a holiday! The call from Deputy Smith had nixed any chance for that.

Zach took a couple of painkillers and swallowed them with the glass of water beside his bed. Moving stiffly, he located his laptop in the den and tried to get comfortable.

He checked his inbox. Yes, true to his word, the deputy had forwarded the information he needed to begin tracing Vince's email. With a prayer for expediency and success, Zach went to work.

* * *

It had taken all night and the better part of the morning to reach the end of the trail. Vince had bounced the email around the world several times before it landed in Cody, Wyoming. A call to Nick with the IP address, and Zach was finally free to crawl back into bed.

He pondered the sense of accomplishment and justice that he had helped to bring about as he pulled the covers up under his chin. It felt good to truly make a difference.

20

"I'm in a deal making mood." Brian leaned back casually in the chair opposite the detainee. "But it'll only last so long." He shrugged nonchalantly. "Tell me who you and your cousin are working for and the DA might consider cutting off some jail time in return for your cooperation."

The interview room was of plain brick, the windows barred and a one-way mirror lined the opposite wall. The warrant to search and apprehend the occupant of a rather elegant country home on the outskirts of Cody had been granted swiftly. Local authorities had swept through the place and seized one Pietro Moretto, who had wisely surrendered to police custody.

The miscreant sat facing Brian at the table in the center of the room. The officer on duty stood beside the window, leaning against the bricks. His arms crossed his chest and his inscrutable gaze studied the prisoner. Pietro Moretto stared right back through dark savvy eyes.

Seeing his tight-lipped response, Brian decided a gentle nudge was in order. "Pete, I admire your loyalty, but your cousin's a dead man walking. Authorities are going to shoot first and ask questions later. You help us and we'll bring him in alive."

More silence.

"Okay, let's review the dirt we've got on you. Your prints match the ones we picked up on the bus where you helped Vince escape. A hair fiber put you in the Walkerville office where you broke him out of police custody. The email Vince sent ties you into his business of identity theft. And finally, the arms we found at your home in Cody were all reported stolen over the course of ten months. Pete, you are going away for a very long time."

A disconcerted light entered his eyes and beads of sweat formed on his brow. Still, he remained mute.

"Whoever your boss is, he's not worth protecting." Brian assessed the mood of the man opposite him. A little more pressure and he might break. "How long is he looking at, Watkins?"

The deputy came away from the wall, his look knowing. He was opening his mouth to reply when Pietro broke his silence.

"You don't get it! Deal or no deal, if I talk, I'm a dead man."

Brian's scrutiny was calm. "We can protect you. You help us and we'll put this guy away for good."

Pietro shook his head, his expression bitter. "No one squeals on my boss. No one." He exhaled and sank back in his chair dejected.

Brian regarded him pensively. Whoever this bigger fish was, identity theft had to be the tip of the iceberg if he could inspire such fear in his people.

* * *

"There's just been some activity on that credit card Vince was using," Deputy Watkins informed his colleague.

The interview had been a dead end. Pietro Moretto was utterly convinced he would die should he cooperate with the law.

"Where?" Brian glanced up from his own desk where he had been staring at a lengthy list of Vince's friends and relatives, trying to figure out where the fugitive might have gone to ground.

"A little airport just outside of Walkerville. Seems he's trying to rent a small plane."

"Call in all units and arm up. Let's nab this guy tonight."

* * *

A police vehicle with lights flashing pulled in front of Vince's rented plane. He spotted several others to the right of the tarmac and clenched his jaw. He thrust the brake on and the small aircraft came to a halt on the runway.

Vince watched officers swarm from their vehicles to surround his plane and he bit back a frustrated curse. His latest identity change clearly hadn't been enough to fool them. It was over, and he was finished.

* * *

Nick smiled with satisfaction and hung up the phone. They had him. He wasn't talking, but at least Vince Moretto was off the streets. Bale had been denied and he was under full guard.

He made a quick call to Logan and Laina to inform them of the good news, and then circled his desk. He grabbed his hat from the stand by the office door and dropped it on his head. Nick pulled the keys to the work car from his pocket. He was due to come off night duty in less than an hour. Things were pretty quiet at the moment, so he planned to catch breakfast with Emily at Gracie's before returning for the changeover of shifts.

Nick exited the office and closed the door. Something bit into his flesh with the punch of a heavy weight champion. Searing pain blinded him as the bullet penetrated his back and thrust him against the glass door. He slumped to the pavement in a state of shock and confusion. He hadn't even heard a gunshot.

As daylight began to fade from his vision, he surrendered his soul to his Savior. There was too much life still to be lived. He wasn't ready, but apparently his time had come.

* * *

Zach heard the door open and glanced from the television screen to the front entrance. His mother was in the kitchen, and the only other person he knew who didn't knock was Laina.

However, standing silently in the hall was a stranger. Zach saw the balaclava and his blood ran cold. He reacted when the man's right arm rose in a decisive move and a handgun pointed at his chest.

Zach grabbed the empty breakfast tray still on his lap and whipped it up as a shield at the same time a muted gunshot sounded. The tray slammed into him. He pulled it away and saw the bullet indentation in the metal only inches from his body. The next shot would not miss.

He flung the tray at the intruder and scrambled from his chair. The tray found its mark, hitting the man in the chin. His arm steadied and aimed.

"Zach, I know you've just eaten but would you like-"

The gunman swung his weapon toward the kitchen doorway. Caroline's eyes widened with terror and she automatically launched the boiling hot water from the pot in her hands. The gunman shrieked in agony and tore at the balaclava now holding the scolding water against his skin.

Zach watched in stunned silence as his mother stepped forward and landed a solid blow with the pot. A loud clang resounded from the intruder's skull colliding with the offending saucepan and he collapsed.

Caroline stared in horror at the man lying on her polished floorboards and then looked at her son.

"Are you alright?"

"Better than him. Good shot, Mom." Zach moved the pistol away with his foot and clutched his aching side. His mending body was protesting his sharp movements.

"That sure put a damper on my plans to cook you the boiled pudding you like."

Zach heard the dry tone in her voice and glanced at his mom in surprise. A shocked laugh escaped his chest. How could she sound calm when his heart was hammering so fiercely he feared it might leap right out of his chest?

"I'll call 911. Here, take this." She handed him the pot.

Zach accepted it in stunned silence and looked down at the man who had moments ago tried to kill him. The burning question, was why?

* * *

Laina was surprised when she had been called in to work. Her boss knew she was in no condition to deal with trauma situations. However, when she understood the extent of the morning's events, she channeled her feelings of horror and revulsion into saving lives. It was nearing midday when she finished and joined Logan's vigil at Walkerville County Hospital.

"How is he?"

Logan rose and drew her into his arms. They stood

in the center of the waiting room, surrounded by other worried friends and family.

"He pulled through surgery. He's being transferred to ICU and then they'll let a few family members in two at a time to see him."

Laina exhaled with relief and leaned into the solid embrace. Nick was going to be okay. By some miracle he had survived a hit man's bullet. However, others hadn't been so lucky.

"Where did Nate send you?" Logan released her and tugged her over to an empty seat by the wall.

Laina saw Emily huddled beside Nick's mother and father. The women's eyes were red and puffy from crying and Emily clutched a handkerchief so tightly in her hands that her knuckles were white.

Laina exchanged a grim glance with Gracie, who had seen the shooting occur right across the street from her diner window. Wil waited quietly beside Gracie, his face ashen.

Laina focused on Logan, who was crouched before her, waiting for an answer.

"There was an explosion at the Walkerville Sheriff's Office. Everyone on duty was killed. Brian Smith, Tyler Watkins, Amy McCall, Randall Dewitt... They're all gone. Nate told me there was a simultaneous attack on the Cody Sheriff's Department. They've lost a lot of good men too."

Logan nodded. Not surprised. He had been watching the breaking news on the T.V in the waiting room. Although it was currently muted, he'd been reading the captions.

"A news presenter said an hour ago that two prisoners in the Cody lockup were found dead this morning. They aren't confirming names yet, but I'd bet my last dollar it's Vince and his partner."

Laina held Logan's sober gaze and had a feeling that this mess was only beginning.

21

"I'm sorry, Zach, I didn't know, or I would have come sooner."

Laina sat opposite her brother at Caroline's kitchen table. Logan sipped his coffee beside her. The woman of the house was just pulling a casserole from the oven.

"I called you over not because I wanted attention, sis'." Zach's gaze leveled on her. "I called you because while we were waiting for the authorities to show up, I found something on the gunman that I thought you ought to know about."

"What was it?" Her brother's grave expression gave her a sense of foreboding and her face drained of color.

Caroline sat a steaming dish on the counter and came to sit with everyone at the table. Laina did not miss the fact that she usually liked to serve food while it was piping hot. What did Zach have to share that was so important Caroline had dropped everything to offer moral support?

"A scrap of paper with an address on it." Zach held her gaze, his own steady. "Yours."

As that shocking piece of information began to sink in, Laina started to feel sick to her stomach.

"You're saying that he was coming for us next?"

Zach exchanged glances with Logan and nodded. Logan gripped her hand on the table top, more for his comfort she supposed than her own, judging by the crushing pressure.

"Let me get this straight," he deducted, "a simultaneous attack takes out the two sheriff offices that have dealt with Vince Moretto, and everybody who has had contact with him or the information he gathered on the USB, is now dead or was on the hit list? Correct me if I'm wrong, but identity theft seems to be the tip of the iceberg here."

Zach sighed and leaned back in his chair. "That's the thought I haven't been able to shake all day."

Righteous anger bubbled inside Laina. She felt wrung out and fed up. It was time to put all of this madness to an end, once and for all. "There's only one way to find out."

All three heads swiveled her direction in surprise. She supposed the steel in her voice might have had something to do with it. Everyone around her seemed to be expecting a meltdown. Well, she was an oak, and it was time to stand up.

"This all began with one man, and it seems to me that ending it all boils down to him as well."

"Who?" the men chimed in unison.

Caroline's perplexed features relaxed. "I know who."

"Vince?" Zach guessed.

Laina shook her head and smiled at her mother. They seemed to be on the same track. "Jamison Harlan."

Zach threw his hands up. "But he's who-knows-where in a coma!"

"Yes, and we're going to find him and pray God wakes him up and gives us some answers."

Logan's lips stretched into a cheeky smile. "I love it when she gets that steely resolve."

Laina's brows flew upward. Caroline slapped her knees decisively and went to serve dinner.

"Since when do you use the words 'steely resolve'?" Zach studied him and an amused smile toyed with his mouth.

"Hey, I'm married to a walking dictionary remember?" Logan winked sideways at his wife.

Laina rolled her eyes and shoved him playfully.

Zach returned to the subject at hand. "So, how do we track down Jamison?"

"There's always a medical trail to follow; prescriptions, equipment, bills. Don't you worry. Wherever Jamison Harlan has gone to ground, we'll find him," Laina assured confidently.

"Preferably before Vince's boss does."

Logan's dry comment was a stark reminder that time was of the essence. They were not the only ones in jeopardy.

* * *

"Did he tell you anything else?" Wil asked, now a man on a mission.

Nick blinked sluggish eyelids and turned to stare at

the ceiling. His brow furrowed in thought. When he spoke, his voice was just barely above a whisper.

"No. I mean I asked about the guy, but he wouldn't speak about him. He said only that he'd died."

Wil frowned. Surely it couldn't all end there? "Which hospital was he at when he passed away?"

"Cody General."

Nick looked spent after only a five minute discussion. His usually tanned skin was pale and pasty, and dark circles rimmed his eyes. Wil was just glad he was going to make it.

"Thanks buddy. Take it easy okay?" Wil patted his arm and received a faint smile in return.

Nick closed his eyes gratefully and slipped back into oblivion. Around him were machines and tubes, all monitoring his vital signs and keeping him pumped full of oxygen, fluids and painkillers.

Wil took it all in and felt anger that whoever had done this was getting away. Sure the shooter had been caught and would be prosecuted to the full extent of the law, but whoever was behind it all, seemed un-traceable.

He silently fumed. "Not if I have anything to say about it!"

* * *

Logan answered the knock on Caroline's front door late that night. Deciding the threat was far from over, they had banded together yet again for safety. He cautiously peered through the peep hole, and seeing it was Wil, he opened the door wide for his friend to enter.

"It's one am. What are you doing here at this hour?"

"I was talking to Nick and he said Jamison Harlan died in Cody General." Wil traipsed straight into the house and through to the kitchen, where he perched on a kitchen stool as though he visited like this every day.

"I phoned the hospital to find out when this was, got a date and the name of the funeral parlor the body was released to. The guy wasn't at all talkative, which I thought was a little strange. He didn't even want to tell me which cemetery Jamison was buried at. Finally after some friendly persuasion, he gave me the name of the place."

Logan stood at the counter and rubbed weary eyes. He had been fast asleep when Wil had knocked.

Caroline appeared in the kitchen from the hallway which led to the family bedrooms. She was wearing a pair of bright yellow pajamas with printed cartoon sheep jumping fences. Logan could not resist a half smile.

"What's going on?"

"Wil's been tracking down Jamison Harlan's final resting place. He apparently died."

Zach wandered in behind his mother and took a seat at the kitchen table. Caroline sighed and put the kettle on.

"So much for that line of inquiry," Zach muttered.

"So much for what line of inquiry?" Laina asked and scuffed sleepily into the room, a pair of Caroline's crazy pink pajamas hanging loosely from her slim frame.

Logan thought she looked adorable. "Harlan's dead."

"Or so people are being led to believe," Wil inserted.

Logan slanted him a suspicious look. "Go on."

"I went to the cemetery and checked out the gravesite. It's just an empty casket."

Caroline's jaw dropped. "You dug up a grave?"

Now the dirt smudges on Wil's checkered shirt and his jeans made sense. Logan grinned and clapped him on the shoulder. Zach snorted in amusement while Laina just shook her head.

"It was dark so nobody saw me, and I covered it over again after I got a look inside."

Wil's placating explanation, aimed at smoothing the look of horror on Caroline's face, managed only to gain a displeased glare.

"So you think Brian Smith had Jamison placed in witness protection?"

"After Vince tried to off him in the hospital, Jamison just disappeared into thin air. I mean, all the hospital staff and records say the same thing; that he never came out of the coma. But that empty grave?" Wil shook his head.

His eyes gleamed with life, and an emotion Logan had rarely seen in him. Anger. He wanted justice. He could well understand. They all did.

"So now that we know Jamison is still alive somewhere out there, how do we find him?"

A slow smile parted Laina's lips. "Just leave that to me, boys."

22

"Are we almost there yet?" Wil whispered from beneath the sheet.

"Sh! You're supposed to be dead, remember?" Laina hissed.

Dressed as an orderly, she wheeled the gurney down a stark white corridor and parked it outside the room they knew would have the key to their search. She slipped inside and began a hasty rummage through filing cabinets. She did not have long. Logan's diversion could only buy her so much time.

There! Jamison's file. She removed it with gloved fingers and carefully closed the drawer. She crept from the room and slipped the file beneath the sheet to Wil. Much further down the hallway she could hear Logan creating a ruckus, demanding Zach's wound be redressed immediately. Most staff had rushed in that direction to assist the nurse on duty with the commotion.

She smiled and wheeled Wil to the elevator. Once safely inside, she paused its progress. Wil sat up and the two of them took half the file each and quickly scanned the pages.

"Chart notes, prescriptions, death certificate-"

"Here, give me that!" Laina snatched the prescriptions.

Wil frowned. "What do you want those for?"

Laina perused the dates each were issued. Some of the medications required authorizations. She smiled when she found the final one. She thrust it into his hand, re-filed the papers and hit the floor they had just come from.

"Lay down."

"Are you going to let me in on why this scrap of paper is so important?"

The elevator dinged and she pushed him down on the gurney, covering him again with the sheet. He complied, albeit with a confused expression. The door opened and she wheeled him back out, parked him against the wall and hurried to replace the file. She could still hear Logan in the background. Quickly in, quickly out.

In minutes she was once again in the elevator with Wil. She dialed Logan's number while Wil rid himself of the hospital garb. He picked up almost immediately, and in the background Laina could hear hospital staff with voices raised.

"We got it. Meet you back at the car."

"Good."

He hung up and she smiled. She could well imagine the scene right now, with Logan suddenly declaring he would take Zach elsewhere. That had been the plan.

She strode with Wil down back passageways and finally out into the car park.

"Now will you tell me why this script is so important?" Wil pestered impatiently.

Laina unlocked the door to his sedan. "Wil, my friend, that prescription is dated the day Jamison died. Now why would a doctor prescribe a dead man painkillers to go?"

Wil's mouth eased into a grin. "So we have more confirmation he's alive. Now what?"

"We visit some chemists and see who is collecting these medications."

* * *

"You should have seen the way Zach played it. He really looked like he was going to pass out, and that red food dye was perfect." Logan grinned at Zach, who laughed.

"And that stink you kicked up about not letting that nurse touch me because she had shifty eyes..." Zach shook his head and smiled. "You were convincing. I actually felt sorry for her."

Logan sobered and let his gaze wander the quiet suburban street. "Yeah, me too. But it was in a good cause."

Wil lifted the binoculars to his eyes and studied the tidy cottage down the quiet suburban street. "I wish I'd been there."

"I could hear enough of it from the hallway," Laina remarked dryly. "Did you two ever think of taking up a career in acting?"

Logan squinted and smiled in satisfaction as the object of their vigil exited the cottage and got into a car. Finding the chemist where the scripts had been dispensed, and the date and times, had helped them gain a description of the woman picking up the medication. Being a local, an elderly store patron had been able to provide them with her name.

"No, but I'm rather liking being a private investigator."

Nick's young deputy, Evan, had caved under the pressure and looked up her name and found an address. With a little digging, they had discovered she was a nurse. She also travelled daily to this small cottage.

"She's leaving," Logan observed.

"So who was that other woman who just entered?" Wil wondered aloud.

"Another nurse paid to relieve her." Laina smiled at Logan. "Come on, let's take a walk and do a little visiting."

He gave her a flirtatious perusal. "Never can say no to a stroll with my pretty wife."

* * *

"You do realize this is trespassing?" Laina whispered and pushed through bushy branches behind Logan.

He peered in the window shrouded by foliage at the side of the cottage. It was high, at least a whole head above her. Logan turned and motioned for her to stand by the wall. He knelt so that she could stand on his knee.

Laina examined the bedroom in a sweeping glance. It was sparsely furnished, except for a built in closet, a comfortable chair, and a bed with a bedside table, both made of nice dark wood. However, the I.V drip beside the sleeping form drew her attention. She studied the male and recognized his face in an instant.

She looked on in astonishment. "It's him! It's Jamison Harlan."

A female entered the room and changed the bag attached to the I.V. She checked other vital signs, all the while talking to the patient, and then sat in the chair with a book.

Laina ducked slowly down so as not to draw attention and beckoned with her finger for Logan to follow her. They quietly extricated themselves from the bushes beside the cottage and circled to the front.

"If we found him this quickly, someone else will too." Logan knocked on the door.

"What are you planning on doing with him anyway?"

"Honestly?" Logan shrugged. "I've no idea. Got any thoughts?"

Laina rolled her eyes. "We should have come up with a plan besides praying he wakes up and tells us what he knows."

"Yeah well, with Deputy Smith being the only one knowing Jamison's whereabouts, and him now dead, I think it's safe to say he's our responsibility for the present. We'll have to come up with a safer place for him, and us for that matter." Logan exchanged glances with her, even as footsteps sounded on the other side of the door and it opened.

23

Logan was opening his mouth to introduce them both when Laina sneezed. The wood of the doorframe splintered behind where her head had been. Logan shoved her inside the cottage and down on the floor. He took the other woman to the ground with him and kicked the door closed.

Laina frowned at him and sat up, rubbing her right elbow. "What was that about?"

"Stay down!"

His barked command sent fear spiraling through her. Several holes appeared in the door above them.

"Someone is shooting at us!"

Laina looked into the frightened brown eyes of Jamison's carer. Her shocked declaration struck Laina like a blow. Another sniper? Had he followed them to Jamison?

"Keep low and follow me," Logan hissed and belly crawled down a central hallway toward the back room where the patient was sleeping.

Laina complied, her head snapping down inches away from polished wooden floorboards as more bullets penetrated and shattered the front windows of the den to their left. One quick glance behind her confirmed that the nurse was on her hands and knees scurrying after them.

"What is going on?" She sounded close to hysteria.

Laina crawled into the back bedroom where Logan was disconnecting the I.V. "Your unconscious friend has been found, that's what's going on."

The bullets stopped. Was the sniper repositioning?

Logan roughly pulled Jamison up and over his shoulder. He carried him unceremoniously through the doorway into the passage to a small kitchen with a back door. Seeing what his plan was, Laina took her cell phone from her pocket and dialed Wil's number.

"Just what do you think you're doing?" The other woman's wide eyes now held a good deal of irritation.

Laina didn't know whether to howl with frustration or laugh. "You can't seriously be worried about what we'll do to him!"

The woman rose from quaking knees onto nervous feet. "Where are you taking him?" She planted her ample frame in the doorway between Logan and the back porch.

"I'm keeping him alive, and if you're smart you'll come with us."

Wil answered her call. "Laina, the shooter is across the street. Go out the back door and try to get to the street behind the one you're on. Zach and I are already on our way."

"Wil, you're a lifesaver!" Laina disconnected the line. "Logan, Wil and Zach will meet us on the street beyond that house." She pointed through the window in the back door to the house beyond a dilapidated, waist high fence.

"And the shooter?"

"Across the street from the front entrance."

Logan pushed past the stunned nurse listening to their rapid exchange onto the veranda. He surveyed the yard for one terrifying second and ran for the back boundary.

Laina grabbed the middle-aged woman by the wrist and hauled her along with them. Logan managed to carefully step over the fence with his long legs, Jamison's limp limbs brushing the weather beaten pickets.

Laina scaled it with the hurdle of an athlete, fueled a great deal by adrenaline. The nurse struggled somewhat, but remained hot on their heels as they charged through the rear yard of the adjoining property.

Laina ran ahead and peered around the house. Wil and Zach were pulling to the curb only a house down from the one they were skirting. "There they are!" She pointed.

Logan passed her, running as fast as he could under his heavy burden. The nurse hesitated.

"My car is back th-"

"Forget your car." Laina snatched her by the wrist again and yanked her past a bed of pansies. She pulled her by some rose bushes onto the front pavement toward the car.

Wil was opening the back door as Logan reached them. Between the two of them, they maneuvered the unconscious man into the rear seat. Laina ushered the flustered nurse into the other side and slid in beside her. Logan squeezed in after Jamison. Wil dove into the passenger seat, seeing as Zach had commandeered the steering wheel.

As soon as the last door had closed, Zach planted his foot on the accelerator.

"Is somebody going to tell me what that was all about back there?" the woman demanded hotly, also doing her best to keep the patient upright and his airway open.

"It's a long story." Logan sighed and passed her a grave look. "You're safer knowing nothing."

"Where do you want us to drop you?" Zach glanced at her in the rearview mirror. "The local sheriff's office or the bus station?"

"If I was you, I'd take the first bus out of town and keep riding until you hit the opposite coast," Logan advised grimly.

Laina scowled at him. "Don't scare her!"

He leaned around the two passengers sandwiched between them. "She *should* be scared. The assassination attempts aren't going to stop until whoever Vince worked for is caught. Jamison holds the key to who that is. Anyone in the way is going to get themselves killed." He shifted his solemn gaze to the terrified woman beside him.

Her hand dropped from holding Jamison upright. Logan pinned him gently back with a powerful forearm, his green eyes softening with compassion.

"I don't want to freak you out, ma'am, but we're all

living on danger's edge. Now you are too. Go visit a distant relative for a few weeks and lay low. Don't ask questions and don't talk to anybody about this guy till you hear something good in the news." He indicated Jamison with a jerk of his head.

Her short dark curls brushed her shoulders as she looked from Logan to Wil, Zach and then Laina with wide eyes. Her gaze rested finally on her patient and her subdued voice was difficult to hear. "Alright."

* * *

"Is someone following us?" Wil twisted in his seat to make certain.

Logan did the same. "Not that I can see. I would have noticed if the same car tailed us for more than a few turns."

Laina glanced at Wil. "Trust me, he would. He can rattle off details about makes and models so fast it scrambles my brain."

Zach grinned cheekily. "Your brain's always been a bit scrambled."

Laina's gaze zeroed in on the back of his head. "We're going to be cooped up in a small cabin in the middle of nowhere for who knows how long. Do you really want to push your luck?"

Zach turned Wil's car onto a quiet dirt track and carefully navigated pot holes that could swallow a tire whole. "What can I say? I don't like life to get boring."

Logan smiled in dry amusement. "No problems there."

Laina watched towering native trees pass her window and could not help but admire the beauty of the wild ranges behind Icy Creek. "How much further is this hunting shack of your grandfather's?"

Wil turned to look at her in the back seat. "Another twenty minutes or so."

"I'm not trying to sound like a killjoy or anything, but what's our plan beyond getting to a safe house?" she wondered aloud. Jamison was going to need medical supplies to last a week or two.

"We'll sit down and talk details when your mom arrives with provisions. Nick's got an around the clock armed guard on him now, thanks to Dan Fisher pulling a few strings," Logan replied pragmatically.

Laina's gaze drifted out her window again. She would feel a whole lot better when they were all together and safe from more assassination attempts.

24

Anne Mathews' stunned gaze returned for a second glance out her car window. She slowed the vehicle and swept the opposite sidewalk with careful scrutiny. Her face drained of color and her heart froze in her chest. Walter Mathews had indeed just exited the local bar in Icy Creek, and was now flirting with a female patron who had exited with him. A half empty bottle was in his free hand, and his other arm was draped around her shoulder. He smiled and said something that made her laugh.

Anne's blood ran cold. She knew the woman. It was the same one he had fooled around with many years ago. She had confronted him about her one night and been beaten to within an inch of her life for it. If Logan hadn't stepped in, she didn't know what would have happened. That was the night Walter had left for good.

Anne had dared to trust that he had changed. Dared to hope that things would be different this time. Tears sprang to her eyes and she made a beeline for Tia's special school. Part of her wished she had never been witness to her husband's betrayal. The other half was grateful she had been spared the heartache she had almost certainly been about to walk into.

As she trudged brokenly up the pathway to the school entrance, she made a few decisions. One would be to do a little behind the scenes investigation to confirm her suspicions. Another was to visit the local attorney.

* * *

Brylie wondered what had possessed her to walk through those huge double doors. Large columns stretched to an arched roof with intricate designs in the molding. Light shone through beautiful stained glass windows onto dark wooden pews. The grandeur in the architecture was stunning, however she noticed very little of it. Brylie was just about to leave when a rusty voice spoke to her right.

"They knew how to build back then, didn't they? The idea was to lift your eyes up and your thoughts heavenward."

Brylie turned to study the old man walking stiffly from the direction of the confessional. His gray hair was closely cropped, his aged face lined in pleasant places, and his eyes a sparkling blue. A priest's collar was the only indication he was clergy. Otherwise his brown cardigan, beige trousers and comfortable leather shoes gave nothing away.

"The question is, does heaven ever look down?"

A pensive expression came over the time weathered face as he considered her question. He moved slowly to a back pew and eased down onto its hard surface. He patted the space beside him in invitation. Brylie hesitated and then decided she had nothing to lose. She sat. He pointed to the large wooden crucifix on the central wall behind the pulpit. An image of Jesus was upon its brutal beams, beaten and wearing a crown of thorns.

"Heaven did."

Brylie's surprised gaze flew from the old priest back to the cross. She had heard the story of Jesus Christ dying, but never had it seemed valid in her own life.

"I thought only really bad people needed what Jesus did."

Sage eyes studied her silently. They seemed to look right into her soul. She shifted uncomfortably. She knew they had glimpsed the shame and the pain buried deep inside there.

"Sin is not unique to only some people and not others. And something tells me you're aware of that."

Brylie's gaze dropped to her purse clutched between white fingertips. She hated to admit it, but she finally saw what Zach had been saying all along. Laina's words rang fresh in her memory.

"You're a beautiful woman Brylie, but you have serious insecurities that have not only ruined your relationship with my brother, but show a deeper spiritual problem that concerns me... You care more for your designer labels and illustrious career than your eternity... The only way for you to know how to truly love Zach, or any person for that matter, is to experience it at the

Cross first for yourself."

Brylie swallowed hard against the lump rising in her throat. Tears blurred her vision of the crucifix. "What have I done?"

The old priest's eyes softened with compassion. "No more than all of us have at one point or another. All have sinned and come short of the glory of God. That is why God's love is so great, in that while we were yet sinners, Christ died for us."

Brylie recognized the Scriptures the clergyman was quoting. She had heard them read in church many times before, but never had she applied them to herself.

"I never knew. I never saw myself as a sinner."

The old man smiled kindly. "A common problem for many of us prideful human beings. God has been gracious to reveal it to you. Now what will you do with it?"

The gentle question rocked Brylie's world. She felt the reality of her sin and hated it. The shame, the embarrassment, the guilt; she wanted rid of it for good! She was tempted to run and bury herself with work and reaching her goals. Yet something told her today's encounter was a once in a lifetime opportunity. If she squandered it, would God come after her again? Or would he simply respect her decision and leave her to live her life as she pleased?

She looked earnestly into the priest's compassionate eyes. "What do I do?"

He smiled warmly. "You're a wise woman, and a courageous one."

Brylie half smiled in derision. "I'm self centered and shallow. I've spent my life climbing over people to get what I want."

"Better to know that now, than waste the rest of your life continuing down that path." He held her gaze, his eyes gentle.

The tension inside Brylie released. "What do I say to God?"

"Tell him exactly what you're thinking. He's waiting with open arms." The gentleman rose, squeezed her shoulder with an arthritic hand, and left her alone.

Brylie's gaze lifted to the cross on the wall and her sin returned to haunt her. "I put You there."

No, I chose the cross so that I might have you.

The strange impression alighted upon her thoughts like a butterfly upon a flower. Tears spilled upon her lashes as abundant love washed over her soul.

Her voice was a whisper. "I'm so sorry for my sin! Please, take all of me?"

I accept.

The gentle words brought forth a smile. For the first time she could ever recall, Brylie felt valued for who she was, regardless of her imperfections. She sighed in deep contentment. It was okay to simply be herself. He loved her.

25

Laina stared pensively out the cabin window. They had been safely ensconced here for a week now and were no closer to the situation being resolved than when they had arrived. She was beginning to wonder if hiding out was a good idea. At least when they were getting shot at they had been gaining answers.

News reports were available via internet on her phone, and they showed that police were looking into a shooting in Walkerville, but were appealing to the public for information. No victims were reported and eyewitness accounts said the gunman had escaped. In other words, they had hit a dead end.

"Maybe we should talk to the FBI or some other government agency." She continued to stare at the stand of enormous pines surrounding the private lake in the small valley below the cabin. Shadows filled their ranks and unnerved her. She hated waiting for trouble to find them.

"About what?"

The unfamiliar male voice caused Laina's heart to lurch. She spun around. There was no one else in the small bedroom off the main living area. It was occupied by a single bed, a shabby bedside table and a beaten up wardrobe. Beside the bed was a wooden chair where she and Caroline had been taking turns watching the patient beneath a quilt. He was attached to a drip and a feeding tube.

Laina's eyes rested upon the comatose man. She jolted in surprise to find Jamison blinking against the late afternoon sun streaming through the window. She scuttled to his side and looked down into his face. He squinted to focus on her and a slow smile stretched his parched lips.

"Wow," he managed in a whisper.

Amusement tugged at Laina's mouth. She wasn't looking her best, but apparently it wasn't bad. "How are you feeling?"

He gave her a lethargic smile. "Better every minute I stare into your beautiful blue eyes."

Laina held up her left hand and her wedding band sparkled. "Sorry. I'm already spoken for."

Jamison grinned and his eyes closed wearily. "Doesn't mean I can't look."

Laina laughed.

Her patient opened his eyes again and allowed his curious gaze to roam the room. "Where am I?"

"Wil's grandfather's cabin. Here, have a sip of water." She took her glass of water from the bedside table and held it for him. With one hand beneath his head and the other holding the glass, he managed to drink. He laid his head back with a tired sigh.

The medic in Laina demanded an answer to her previous question. "How are you feeling?"

His eyes closed. "Like I could sleep for a week."

She wondered if his injury had caused any disabilities or memory loss. "Can you tell me your name?"

"Jamison Harlan." He squinted at her. "Who is Wil?"

Laina's smile was a relaxed one. There was obviously no trouble with his short term memory. "I'll call the guys in a minute. First I want to make sure you're okay. When they find out you're awake, you won't get a moment's rest."

He frowned at her in puzzlement. "How long have I been asleep?"

Laina's look was wry. "Long enough for me to get married and a few assassins to wreak havoc in our county."

Jamison's eyes snapped with keen intelligence. "Who are you?"

"I'm Laina Mathews. We met on the prison bus. I helped pull you from the wreck. That's how this all started."

"I'm listening."

* * *

"So who is this guy you and Vince were working for?" Zach asked the question they had all been chewing over for weeks.

He was sitting on the end of Jamison's bed. The patient was upright and leaning against a stack of pillows. He looked positively worn out. Caroline had managed to get some soup into him and was now holding his empty bowl and sitting in the chair by his bed.

Wil had carried in a rocker from the main room and was listening pensively from his seat beside Caroline. Logan was leaning against the window ledge, arms crossed and mind looking like it was ticking over at a thousand revs per minute. Laina had cleared the bed-side table and made that her perch for the lengthy conversation since the patient had awakened.

"His name is Mason Carter." Jamison appeared to force heavy eyelids open. "He's a successful business-man who lives in Cody. It took awhile to dig up infor-mation on him, but I finally found out that his birth name was Abdul Parham. He moved to the US as a teen from Iran. He's now in his late 50's and very much an Al Qaida sympathizer.

"He had Vince and me stealing identities that were being used to help foreigners gain illegal entry into the country. It's my belief he's setting up terrorist cells."

Zach was astounded. "This is about terrorism?"

"If that's the case, then something big is being planned."

Wil studied Logan with unease. "What makes you say that?"

"Every person who has any knowledge of Vince and the identity thefts has been targeted for assassination. We're the only ones left, and then only by the grace of God."

"You need to contact the department of homeland security," Jamison stated quietly. His head leaned back against the pillows behind him and his eyes closed of their own volition.

"Alright boys, it's time to leave the poor man alone to get some rest." Caroline rose and shooed them all toward the door.

"Laina, can I use your phone?" Logan pushed away from the window sill and held out his hand in anticipation.

"Sure." Laina removed her mobile from her pocket as they filed from the room and passed it to him. "Calling the FBI?"

"Yeah. This thing is bigger than county police."

"That's an understatement."

* * *

It was the law of sowing and reaping. Anne understood that now. It had taken many years to come to grips with the fact she had been allowing her husband's lack of personal growth to persist. If she had set boundaries to protect herself and her children, maybe he would have realized sooner the wrongness of his behavior. In the end, Logan had done it for her.

Anne sipped her cup of coffee at the kitchen table and watched Tia slowly pick her way through her evening meal. In retrospect, Walter still expected her to comply with everything he wanted, even if his treatment of them was vastly improved.

I'd rather be alone and living peacefully than in a sit-

uation where I'm fighting for my freedom all the time.

Judging by what she had seen that afternoon, all of Walter's talk about Christianity and following Jesus was just another ploy to get her to allow him to come home. She had seen the difference Jesus could make in a life. Logan had undergone some serious changes since his conversion as a teenager. She smiled when she thought of what a lovely young man her son had become.

God, I've watched Logan for many years, and what he's got with You is genuine. I'd like that too.

Anne sat her cup on the table and smiled with the peace she felt upon making that decision. She thought of her next choice and drew a fortifying breath.

God, I hope You'll forgive me. I'll never marry again if that's what it takes to honor my vows. But I can't go back to the way things were. It's time I faced reality and made my separation from Walter official.

Somehow she knew God would understand. Walter had sown his choices, and if he was to ever grow, he needed to reap the consequences.

26

Laina met Logan at the cabin door. "What did they say?"

He handed her phone over and collected Wil's keys from the crude table just inside the door. He had stepped outside where reception was a little better to make the phone call. Laina had just returned from checking on Jamison.

"How is he?" Logan nodded toward the bedroom.

"He's sleeping." She waited expectantly.

Logan seemed reluctant. "They want to discuss it in person. They also want to see the USB. Zach and I are going to drive into town to meet them. You guys should be fine with Wil and your mom here. I hear Mom packs a mean wallop with a pot." A cheeky smile revealed a row of white teeth.

Laina was not amused. "And if the sniper is still looking for Jamison and recognizes you in town?"

"We'll have an FBI agent or two on our side this time." Seeing she was unconvinced, he gently cupped her cheek with a large work roughened hand. "We'll be okay, Ace. Keep the place locked and stay inside. We'll be back in a couple of hours."

He leaned down and kissed her softly. Laina's senses

heightened and a tingle ran down to her toes. She smiled blissfully.

"That was nice."

"Just a taste of things to come." He touched her nose with his index finger and grinned.

Laina conceded defeat. "Be safe."

Logan glanced over her head into the room. "Zach, get your computer stuff. We're heading into town. Wil, come see us off."

The boys scrambled into action and pushed past Laina. She frowned. What parting discussion was Logan planning on having with Wil? She shook her head and went to make a cup of coffee. She didn't want to know.

* * *

Finding Jamison had been straightforward. He smiled in sadistic pleasure at how easy this was going to be. The woman and her friends were all together, like cattle in one pen ready for the slaughter. The woman, her husband, her mother, her brother and friend were on his list along with Jamison. Gaining the information had been relatively simple. Find the woman, and he would find Jamison and the others.

It was a seemingly small mistake to make really. The average person did not think of such things, and that's what he had counted on. All it had taken was getting her cell phone number, an uncomplicated process of talking with her employer using a convincing pretext.

Then he had traced her location using the GPS in her phone.

This time he would not fail. He could not afford to. His boss was not a tolerant man. He slunk through the woods to the west of the small cabin in search of a suitable spot. He was only yards from the perfect place when movement caught his eye. A car was leaving.

Frustration rose within him. He looked through his rifle scope and counted only two people inside the vehicle. He settled in to wait. With four still remaining, he had plenty of work to do, and the other two would no doubt return. When they did, it would be to a scene totally different to the one they had left.

* * *

Logan and Zach waited inside Gracie's diner in a corner booth. Logan had chosen it specifically because it allowed them to see everyone and keep their backs to the wall. It wasn't long before two men entered.

Everything about them screamed FBI. The men were wearing dark suits and crisp shirts. Polished shoes peaked from beneath dress slacks. Each pair of eyes calmly assessed the occupants in the diner and finally locked with Logan's. His cool evaluation seemed to draw their keen attention. He lifted a hand and nodded in greeting. They approached.

The taller of the two men, a touch shorter than six foot, outstretched his hand. Dark closely cropped hair framed an interesting face. He appeared to be in his late thirties to early forties. Guarded brown eyes appraised Logan and then Zach. Logan shook the offered hand.

"Ryan Miller, FBI." He removed his wallet from an inner jacket pocket and flashed his credentials.

"Logan Mathews."

He extended his hand to Zach, who returned the greeting. "Zach Delaney."

The second gentleman, who was of average height and build, offered his hand and the men shook. Where his partner had dark hair, his was fair. "Geoffrey Wellard."

They slid into the booth opposite Logan and Zach. Logan did not miss the way they too positioned themselves so that they could see the room.

"So, tell us about this Mason Carter, formerly Abdul Parham. He's not on our watch list."

"Well he aughta be." Logan tapped Zach's laptop, which lay on the table between them. "We've got something you need to see."

* * *

Wil wandered from the lake with a string of fresh fish and a contented feeling in his soul. Laina smiled at him from the doorway of the cabin.

"I wish you'd have told me you were going fishing. I'd have come with you."

He grinned. "And risk you out-fishing me?"

Laina laughed.

Wil leaned his pole against the log wall. He glanced up at her and frowned. There was a red dot moving up her body and honing in on her forehead. Wil's heart leapt into his throat and he acted without thought. He body tackled her in the doorway. Glass in a picture frame on the mantel piece on the far wall shattered. They both landed on the wooden floor with a thud.

"Wil, are you mad?" Laina blinked, as though she was seeing stars after the collision.

Wil glanced up and saw that a bullet hole remained in the picture above the fireplace. He rolled off Laina and onto his side in one fluid movement and yanked the cabin door shut.

"What has gotten into you?" She sat up and rubbed the back of her head.

"Sniper." He crawled to the window and chanced a peek over the frame.

Laina's eyes widened in horror and she flattened herself against the floor on her stomach. Caroline chose that moment to walk into the main living area from Jamison's room.

"What is going on out here?"

"Mom, get down!"

Caroline's gaze swept the room and alarm filled her countenance. She dropped to the floor. "He's here?"

Wil slid down the wall away from the window and sat with his legs bent at the knees. "It's my guess he's on the west side of the lake."

Laina frowned at him. "How do you figure that?"

Wil's gaze cast about the cabin. "With the angle that bullet came into the cabin, he's not shooting directly head on." He pointed to the mantel and the shattered photo frame. It was slightly in and to the right of the doorway. "The land on the west of the lake is high ground. It's where I'd pick if I was hunting, and it's downwind of the cabin today."

Laina shook her head. "What do we do?"

"Call 911." Caroline's gaze went between the two north facing windows looking out on the lake.

Laina pulled her cell phone from her jeans pocket and cringed. "No network. The only spot it gets a signal is out in the yard, fifty or so feet from the cabin."

Caroline rolled her eyes. "Does anything ever go right for us?"

"Laina could be dead right now. I'd say my tackle was a success." Wil glanced at her.

Laina could not resist a small smile. "You charge like a linebacker."

Wil spotted his grandfather's antique flintlock rifle above the door and his mind formulated a plan. He rose out of sight of the windows and snatched it from its brace.

Laina scowled at him. "You had better not be planning on doing what I think you're doing."

Wil ignored her look and crawled to the back exit. "Keep away from the windows and grab Jamison. All of you get down into the cellar. The trap door is in the kitchen beside the old stove." He turned to pass the women a serious warning glance. "Whatever you hear, *do not* come out."

Fear crept into Laina's wide blue eyes. She looked haunted as Wil snuck out the back door and disappeared into the woods behind his grandfather's cabin.

27

"We'll get on this straight away. Thank you both for your time."

Logan's gaze followed Agent Wellard. He had listened to their spiel, shared a glance with his partner and slipped from the booth to go make a phone call. He was just outside the diner and Logan watched him through the window.

"That's good news." Zach closed his laptop and handed over the USB. "But what about us? The hit men aren't going to stop coming until you have evidence enough to haul Mason Carter in."

"We're coming with you." Agent Miller stated this as though his informants had assumed this were the case. "We'll be placing Jamison Harlan in protective custody today, and will have you and your friends under tight surveillance until this case is resolved."

"Oh."

Logan watched the other agent drop his phone back into his jacket pocket and re-enter the diner. "Jamison ought to be evidence enough."

Agent Miller's smile was business-like as he gestured for them to precede him. "We'll find out shortly, won't we?"

* * *

Wil crouched and slowly scanned the terrain. He had skirted around the cabin to the west on stealthy feet. He mentally thanked his grandfather for all of the hunting trips they had gone on when he was a boy. Knowing how to move silently through the thick stand of trees and what to look for when tracking prey, were skills he had always taken for granted. Now his life depended on them.

The native pines reached heavenward, their needles whispering in a gentle breeze. He was upwind of where he guessed the shooter had been. He would have moved when his first shot failed, unless he was sure his targets were unarmed and without assistance. A quiet scraping sound drifted on the wind to Wil's sensitive ears. His gaze snapped to the left and down the slope.

Low lying shrubbery dotted grassy gaps between the trees. His sharp vision narrowed in on a patch of crushed grass behind a small outcropping of rocks. It had to be the place from where the shot had been taken. It was along the edge of the tree line and had excellent visibility.

The sniper was repositioning, but slowly so as not to draw attention to his movements. Wil crept carefully to his left, listening intently. The trail of crushed grass showed that the sniper was crawling low to the ground. Wil stopped.

He could see the heel of a boot beneath a shrub ten feet below him. His heart hammered in his chest. The place the sniper had chosen was exactly where he would have picked. The cabin was one hundred and fifty yards below. This time his position allowed him to see the back door as well as the front. Wil was glad he had come out before the sniper had moved, or he would have been a sitting duck.

Wil did a thorough scan to ensure the gunman was alone. He raised his grandfather's flintlock rifle to his shoulder and moved steadily downhill. He halted several feet away.

"I'd like it if you'd kindly take your hands off your weapon and move out of there so I can see you." Wil's calm tone gave no hint to the fear spiralling through him.

The boot jolted slightly and then the figure lay still. Wil loudly cocked the hammer. The villain took the wordless message seriously and slowly crawled from beneath the shrub, leaving his rifle where it was. Wil could see the butt of a formidable weapon. It looked professional. His mouth suddenly felt dry.

Cold brown eyes assessed the antique firearm and then met Wil's hard stare. The gunman was Caucasian, of average height and wiry build. His light colored hair was closely cropped in military style and he wore hunters' camouflage shirt and trousers.

"Now stand up slowly."

Skeptical eyes glanced at the flintlock rifle. "There's no way that relic is loaded."

The rifle was from 1825 and only worked with powder and shot, of which he had none. Wil's hands trembled slightly with adrenaline.

The corner of the sniper's mouth twitched in a sadistic smile. "Even if it was loaded, what are the chances it will even work?" He stood in slow, careful movements. He was calling Wil's bluff.

Wil spotted the handle of a hunting knife protruding from the other man's left boot and immediately saw his intention. The knowledge that this man had tried to kill them twice was enough to chase away his fear.

In a lightening quick move, the hardened killer drew his knife and lunged. Wil deflected the blade downward with his barrel. A split second later he kicked the miscreant in the face while he was bent. The man fell backward, the knife flying loose. He landed near his own rifle. He was reaching for it when the butt of Wil's gun connected with his skull.

Wil stared in cold anger at the unconscious man sprawled on the ground. "It works just fine thanks."

* * *

"It's safe to come out!"

Laina's eyes closed against tears and she exhaled in relief at the sound of Wil's voice. She dropped the pot in her hands and ascended the stairs from the cellar. Caroline helped Jamison onto unsteady legs and followed more slowly. Laina cleared the cellar entrance and crossed the main room. She flung open the cabin door and froze.

She stared in shock as her usually gentle friend carelessly dropped an unconscious man on the ground like a sack of grain. Blood seeped from a knock to his head and leaked steadily into the dust in which he was lying. Laina's stunned gaze lifted to Wil's face, where she read fury.

She wiped damp palms on her jeans. "Are you alright?"

"You can go find a signal with your phone now." He brushed past her into the cabin and re-hung his grandfather's rifle.

Laina bent to check if the man had a pulse. Strong and stable. Breathing shallow but steady. Wil returned and knelt at her side with a rope. He began to roughly bind the sniper's hands and feet. She decided it might be wise to get out of his way.

Caroline put her arm around Laina's shoulder and held out her free hand. Laina passed her the mobile phone. Jamison leaned against the cabin doorframe for support and watched the goings on while Caroline wandered down the yard to dial 911.

"I'm going for a walk. I'll be down by the lake." With that, Wil stood and strode toward the water sparkling in warm sunshine two hundred yards away.

Laina mouthed a silent whoa and watched him go in astounded silence.

28

The FBI agent closed the door to the backseat of their vehicle. Inside was the hit man, conscious, cuffed, head bandaged and glaring at him.

"If looks could kill." Logan smiled in amusement at Agent Miller.

A corner of the officer's mouth lifted in response and his eyes lit with enjoyment. Justice was clearly satisfying. Logan's arms came around Laina. His embrace was a safe haven after the storm.

She hugged him fiercely in return. "What now?"

"He'll be interrogated. We've already got agents on Mason Carter. He'll be in custody within the hour." Agent Wellard seemed distracted as he answered. His focus was on the sniper's cell phone in his hand.

"How did he find us way out here?" Caroline asked in bewilderment.

Zach placed a protective arm around her shoulders.

Agent Miller looked around the circle of friends standing near his vehicle. "Anyone got a mobile on them?"

Laina frowned in puzzlement. "Yeah, me."

His look was pragmatic. "He likely traced your location by the GPS in your phone. All he would need is your number."

Laina swallowed hard. She had almost gotten them all killed.

"It's okay, Ace. It's not your fault." Logan gave her a gentle squeeze.

"Yeah, I should have thought of it." Zach glanced at her apologetically. "You weren't to know."

"What happens to Jamison now?" Caroline met the easygoing gaze of the man she had helped nurse.

"I'll probably end up in witness protection until this is all over." He shrugged reasonably. "It's better than being six-foot under."

Caroline's worried gaze held his. "You just remember what we spoke about."

Jamison smiled warmly. "Yes ma'am."

Zach looked at her curiously. His expression held the question Laina was wondering. What had they discussed?

Agent Wellard frowned. He passed the phone to Agent Miller.

His brows shot up and he handed the mobile back to his partner. "Reply."

With his eyes intense, Wellard began texting.

"What is it?" Jamison indicated the sniper's phone inquisitively.

"There's a message that says: 'Have the targets been acquired?'" Agent Miller informed them.

"And what's your answer?" Logan asked the lawman texting.

Agent Wellard hit send. "'Targets eliminated.' That

should buy you all some peace and quiet." He nodded toward the prisoner. "By the time whoever sent him finds out you're alive, they'll be in custody too and unable to send anyone else." He turned to his partner. "Let's get a trace on this number."

"I'll call it in. Jamison, gather your things. We need to get this reprobate back to headquarters."

"What happens to us?" Wil finally broke into the conversation.

"We'll need your statements," Agent Wellard answered. "This place will be crawling with FBI and county police in minutes."

"You'll be put under protective surveillance until this is resolved," Agent Miller added calmly.

Laina sighed. "And I thought this was over."

Jamison winked at her. "It's just beginning."

* * *

Logan's arm slipped around Laina's shoulders and she leaned against him, dropping her head to his shoulder. They were sitting on the grassy bank of the lake, watching as the setting sun cast an orange glow upon its rippling surface. Behind them, the county police and FBI teams were wrapping up their investigation.

Wil was sitting nearby with a line dropped in the water. Beside him was a string of fish. Laina was still marveling over the different side to him she had seen that afternoon. This image, calm, quiet and gentle was the one she was used to. The other, righteous indignation and swift justice, was astounding.

Zach had remained up at the house with Caroline. Last Laina had seen them, they were drinking coffee and talking in depth perched on a small boulder to the side of the cabin.

Laina heard footsteps and both she and Logan glanced behind them. An FBI agent they had been introduced to as Rebecca Swanston, crouched beside them.

She offered a smile. "Thanks for your patience."

Laina gestured to the sunset. "Not exactly hard to do when you've got this vista."

Agent Swanston chuckled. "There is that."

Logan studied her carefully, seeming to gauge what news they were about to receive. Wil glanced up from the rod in his hands, silently waiting.

Seeing the expectant eyes on her, Rebecca got straight to matters at hand. "You're all free to go. We've collected enough evidence for ballistics reports and your statements all match up. An agent will accompany Caroline and Zach, Wil, and the both of you to your respective homes."

"I hope he or she likes takeout, 'cos I'm not in the mood to cook," Laina joked.

Rebecca grinned. "That sounds like a plan."

Logan frowned. "The guy who sent the hit men knows where each of us lives."

Agent Swanston nodded in understanding. "This is just a precaution. We believe the threat is gone. Without going into too much detail, Mason Carter was arrested and will not be receiving bale.

"The search of his home today produced enough evidence to not only put him away for life, but revealed the identities and whereabouts of several terrorist cells throughout the Midwest, and also two along the east coast. We believe they were only days away from enacting a coordinated attack. And with Jamison Harlan's testimony as well..." She shrugged and left the reassuring thought dangling.

Hope lit Laina's tired eyes. "It's over?"

Rebecca's smile was kind. "Yes, it's over." Her gaze encompassed all of them. "You've done an amazing job staying alive and digging for the truth. You'd make good agents."

Wil stifled a wry laugh. "No thanks."

Logan laughed and Laina passed Wil a grin.

"An understandable sentiment." Agent Swanston smiled in amusement and stood.

Laina snuggled into Logan's side and he held her close. Their eyes drifted again to the sun dipping below the tree covered mountains beyond the lake.

"Anything biting Wil?"

"Nope. They must've got wind of you. When was the last time you showered?"

Logan sniffed his underarm. "Come on, I'm not that bad."

Wil wore a deadpan. "You know what they say about the fox and its own scent."

Laina's shoulders shook with silent laughter.

Agent Swanston looked puzzled. "You are free to go, remember?"

Laina smiled lazily up at her. "We know."

The other woman smiled and shook her head. She turned and wandered toward the cabin and the circle of vehicles now beginning to fill with lawmen.

Wil jerked his rod upward.

"Got a bite?"

"Yeah, maybe the fish are downwind of you."

Logan smiled, amused. "Hey, be nice or I might not offer to cook those over the fire tonight."

Laina turned slightly to look into his handsome face. "We're staying for dinner?"

"Can't let a good string of fish go to waste."

She smiled in pure contentment and gave him a squeeze. Wil reeled in another trout and passed them both a grin.

Logan dropped a kiss on her lips and suddenly rose. "I'll go build a fire and fetch the skillet."

"I'll tell Mom and Zach our plans."

"And don't forget our FBI dinner guests."

"I won't."

Her heart warmed at the prospect of a relaxed evening eating together over a campfire. It was a fitting celebration to conclude a tempestuous few weeks.

EPILOGUE

Laina glanced up with the jingle of the bell above the diner door. Her anxious gaze followed Logan as he crossed the room and joined them at their favorite corner booth.

He passed Caroline a warm smile and punched Zach lightly in his good arm. Zach cringed anyway. The healing process was well underway, but not entirely at its completion.

"How was your day, Mom?" he asked his mother-in-law easily.

Caroline's gaze was also anxious as she waited for news. "How is she?"

"Yeah, how did it go?"

Logan sighed and fiddled with a salt shaker. "He took it better than I thought he would. I mean, he got angry, but he didn't get violent."

"And your mom?" Zach prompted.

"She handled it well, all things considered. She was peaceful and planning on taking Tia to the park when I left."

Laina thought back on her recent conversation with Anne Mathews. It had been both joyous and sad at the same time. Her mother-in-law had confided that she had begun a relationship with Jesus Christ. Moments later she explained her decision to officially divorce Walter Mathews. The two seemed so contrary, but Laina understood. It was one thing to love and forgive, and another to put yourself and your family back into an unhealthy situation.

According to Anne, and some of what her attorney had found out, Walter had been using the pretext of being a new convert to Christianity in order to gain her trust, and subsequently her help with his mounting debts. Logan had not seemed surprised, although he had been disappointed.

"And your dad?" Caroline asked softly.

Laina marveled at her mother's ability to show compassion when the man had tried to deceive them all.

Logan nodded calmly. "He was shocked at first and then angry. He cooled quickly though. I think he knew he had it coming. I spoke with him when we left Mom's. I didn't hold back on the truth, and he did seem genuinely sorry. He asked if he could still keep in touch with me."

Laina opened her mouth to protest. Logan seemed to read her thoughts and jumped in to reassure her.

"I told him outright he had to solve his money problems by himself, but he could keep in touch if that was what he wanted. I also gave him the name and number of our pastor and an elder at church who runs an AA group if he was really interested in changing." Logan shrugged. "For what it's worth, he took it."

Caroline smiled hopefully. "That's good."

Logan met her gaze. "I thought so."

Laina nudged her husband with her shoulder. "I'm proud of you."

He draped an arm around her shoulder and gave her a kiss. His eyes gleamed cheekily and passed appreciatively over her soft pink top and fitted denim jeans. "I'm kinda proud o' you too Ace. You're the second best lookin' woman in this diner."

Laina raised one brow. "The second best?"

He passed Caroline a grin. "Your mom's the first."

The woman in question chuckled. "I like a son who knows how to butter up his mother-in-law. You've married a very wise man, Laina."

Laina slid a warning glance at Logan. "We'll see."

Zach suddenly changed the subject. "Hey, has anyone heard anything about Jamison?"

"Nope, he's disappeared into the woodworks. I'm sure he'll resurface when the trial is finished. There's no way Carter is getting away with all he's done. It'll be a miracle if he doesn't get the death penalty," Logan surmised.

Laina remembered an earlier conversation between Jamison and her mother and looked at her curiously. "What did you talk about with Jamison?"

"Which discussion in particular?"

Zach's eyes lit with interest. "Yeah, just before he left the cabin you referred to a conversation you'd had."

Caroline smiled. "Ah yes. I told Jamison in no uncertain terms that he had almost died twice and asked if he had given any thought to his eternity."

Laina was surprised at her mother's bluntness. "What did he say?"

"He said he believed in God but didn't honestly know much about Him. We had a great chat about Jesus and God's plan to rescue each of us personally."

"Did he make a decision?"

Caroline smiled sagely at her daughter. "You know such weighty matters take time and consideration. That's why I urged him to think about it."

Laina accepted at her logic with a shrug.

"Hey, did I tell you guys I got a call from Brylie?" Zach spoke up.

Both Caroline and Laina studied him warily. Laina couldn't help but wonder what scheme his ex-girlfriend might be up to. Logan seemed a little more nonchalant.

"Does she still hate your guts?"

Laina leveled her husband with a disapproving stare. Logan only grinned at her.

Zach chuckled. "Actually no. She apologized. Laina apparently said some things that made her take stock of her life. She's gotten serious about God and is moving on in leaps and bounds. She said to pass on her apologies for her behavior and to say thanks for your prayers and kindness."

Laina sat back against the booth in stunned silence.

Caroline took in her reaction with an amused expression. "How faithless we often are. We pray God will reach a person and are surprised when He actually goes ahead and does it."

Laina marked an imaginary scoreboard. "One to you,

Mom."

Logan laughed softly and took a drink of Zach's soda. Zach ignored him and sat a little straighter, his gaze trained upon the other side of the room. His face lit with excitement. "Guys, he's here."

Each head swiveled in the direction of the diner entrance where Wil was holding open the door for Emily and Nick. She pushed him in his wheelchair, carefully navigating the tables to cheers from the crowd who had gathered to celebrate his release from hospital that day.

Nick, although pale and visibly weary, smiled in pleasure at the show of love and acceptance from the townsfolk he served. Dan Fisher was among them, also not yet up to strength, but looking better than when Laina had last seen him.

Emily parked Nick at the table beside theirs where his parents were seated.

"How'd you get out so soon?" Logan teased. "Did the nurses get sick of your whining?"

Nick's lips tipped up at the corners in amusement. "Seems so. What's this I hear about you guys helping put away a terrorist?"

"Those rumors have been greatly exaggerated," Zach joined the jesting.

"So Nick, when do you go back on duty?" Laina asked.

"Not for quite some time if I have anything to say about it." Emily passed her intended a meaningful stare and Nick shrugged and smiled in contentment.

The table erupted in laughter.

Nick met Zach's gaze. "Is it true?"

Logan glanced between them curiously. "Is what true?"

Nick's eyes carried a gleam. "You liked working for the good guys and are considering a career in the cybercrime unit?"

An enigmatic smile toyed with Zach's lips. "Who told you?"

"Oh, just a little bird somewhere along the grapevine."

"I forgot about small towns and gossip."

Logan grinned. "That's as good as a confession."

An adorable hopeful light entered Caroline's brown eyes. "So we might have you around more often?"

"It seems so."

Laina saw the way he tried to hide his pleasure behind an unruffled facade. She smiled knowingly and squeezed Logan's hand under the table. She was equally delighted to have her brother home permanently.

Logan reserved a warm smile just for her and her heart melted a little around the edges. While banter spread back and forth like wildfire, she quietly thanked God for the wonders He had wrought in her life. Jamison had been right. This was just the beginning.

Dear Reader,

I hope you enjoyed reading this story as much as I did writing it. It was fun shifting forward in time from *Where The Heart Belongs* to see what had become of the characters we had come to know as teenagers.

As a reader, we choose exciting stories generally because our lives are not nearly so action packed, and we want to check out of reality for a little while. Whatever our reality may be, the lessons the characters learn through their circumstances are eternal ones that can most certainly apply to our lives.

I've been challenged by God this year to become like an oak tree, steady, unmovable and of blessing to others. Only those in my life will be able to tell you if I've been successful, but then I'm a work in progress. We all are.

At times life can be so stressful, often overcast by pain and adversity. Scripture tells us to be good soldiers of Christ and to endure hardship. (I've got to admit that I don't always like this verse, and try to avoid it. However God keeps taking me back.)

To run from the tough times in our lives is to forfeit greater depth in our relationship with God, and a character that more resembles His own. It's hard, but I've decided to take off my running shoes. The results are slow in coming, but are well worth the effort.

Yet at all times I'm learning that it is imperative to keep the hope of heaven at the forefront of my thoughts. The promise in Revelation that God will one day wipe away all of our tears, and that there will be no more pain, or sorrow, or death, is truly priceless. It gives strength when you feel like giving up, and hope when all seems bleak. It is indeed a reality, and one to be cherished.

So like Laina, will you take up the challenge to become like a mighty oak? Will you allow God to put your roots down deep in Him? Will His every word be your nourishment, causing you to grow and to stand firm in His ways? If that is the case, then you will be a tree of righteousness, the planting of the Lord, and He will be glorified.

Others will find rest in your shade, and food in the fruit of His Spirit in your life (like acorns to a squirrel). You will be resistant to the fire storms that life brings, and in turn will be a shield for those around you. It's certainly something to aspire to, isn't it? You just need to be willing for God to do the work in you.

So, will you take off your running shoes with me? I'm planted, my roots are down and I'm growing (however slowly that may be). Come join me and become an oak.

Love in our great God,

Jo His Daughter

www.jayhdee.weebly.com

www.ingramcontent.com/pod-product-compliance
Lightning Source LLC
Chambersburg PA
CBHW060909250626
47159CB00008B/2937